"You're a ve
Charlie."

Harry was touch
elicited so many

She gazed at him hopefully. "Then..."

"But I'm not going to get involved with you," he said with conviction. "It has nothing to do with you, and everything to do with me. Okay?"

"No."

"Charlie..."

She laughed, because he looked so frustrated. She decided a dose of honesty couldn't hurt. "I want you, Harry. And I'm used to fighting for what I want." When his eyes nearly crossed, she said, "Go ahead and sigh if you really need to, but it won't change anything. Consider yourself forewarned."

He shook his head, then chuckled. "Only you, Charlie, could make a seduction sound like a threat."

She tried for a seductive look and when he didn't laugh she considered herself more successful than not. "I prefer to think of it as a promise, Harry."

Dear Reader,

Harry Lonnigan is a different type of hero for me. Writing him was a challenge in many ways, but not in the most important one. When it came to loving the heroine, Harry knew just what to do. After all, all heroes *do* have a few things in common. And Harry is one helluva guy!

I hope you'll like him and his story as much as I do. Let me know what you think!

You can contact me at P.O. Box 854, Ross OH 45061, or e-mail me at lorifoster@poboxes.com

All the best,

Lori Foster

P.S. Look for my first Harlequin Duets novel, #23 *Say Yes,* on sale March 2000!

Books by Lori Foster

HARLEQUIN TEMPTATION

Lori Foster
In Too Deep

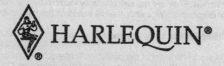

HARLEQUIN®

TORONTO • NEW YORK • LONDON
AMSTERDAM • PARIS • SYDNEY • HAMBURG
STOCKHOLM • ATHENS • TOKYO • MILAN • MADRID
PRAGUE • WARSAW • BUDAPEST • AUCKLAND

To Malle Vallik.
Though you'll no longer be editing at Temptation,
you'll be forever remembered as "one of the great
ones." I take comfort in the fact that your Temptation
novels will go on, pleasing readers for years to come.

ISBN 0-373-25870-4

IN TOO DEEP

Copyright © 2000 by Lori Foster.

Visit us at www.romance.net

Printed in U.S.A.

1

SHE HAD THE soft, sweet mouth of a woman. And as she bent slightly at the waist, peeking out the front window of the quaint grocery shop, he inspected her bottom—and found it equally sweet. His palms itched, and he wasn't certain if it was with the need to caress—or swat.

Maybe she was a cross-dresser. Or she just had really bad taste in clothes. But she was definitely female, of that Harry was certain. He hadn't even noticed her until she'd gotten too close to him, and then he'd picked up on her scent. It made him feel like a buck in mating season, it hit him so hard. He stared, unable to help himself, until she noticed he was staring. Then she gave him a sour look and moved away.

And still he stared. The battered brown leather jacket was a couple sizes too big, ripped at one shoulder seam. And the flannel beneath it was baggy and hanging loose over ill-fitting, patched jeans. Scuffed, low-heel boots with chains on the back gave the impression she was trying for a bad-boy biker look. *Absurd.* Even her slicked back, glossy dark hair, held in a short blunt ponytail at her nape looked more female than rebel male. She had only one pierced ear, a small spent bullet dangling from the tiny silver hoop.

She kept her hands in her back pockets and a sneer

on her face. Harry wondered what she'd done with her breasts, for they weren't noticeable through the bulky clothing. Of course, maybe she was naturally small. He wouldn't mind. He was a bottom-man himself, and he liked petite women, he...

Harry drew up short, appalled at the direction his wandering mind had taken. He wanted nothing to do with the woman, absolutely nothing.

Whatever her excuse for aping a man, she didn't need to be here now, at this precise moment, possibly screwing things up for him, definitely distracting him.

Harry Lonnigan eyed the unfortunate female with annoyance, now dividing his attention between her and the two men working their way to the cash register. He had a job to attend to. Yet there she was, trying to saunter like a man, trying to sneer in a manly way. Harry snorted, then despite himself, he breathed deeply, trying to detect her sweet scent again. Not the smell of perfume, but the smell of warm woman, a smell proven to drive men crazy.

He wanted to ignore her, but couldn't. Who was she and what was she up to with her outrageous costume and bizarre acting? Only a complete imbecile would believe her to be male.

But just then one of the two men turned, eyed her, and gave credence to her costume by dismissing her without so much as a raised eyebrow. Harry was stupefied.

He came out from behind the rack of chips and strolled casually forward, in no hurry to draw attention to himself, but the female was getting entirely too close to the two men, trying it seemed, to keep surveillance out the front display window without being seen. Whatever she was up to, she apparently wasn't aware of the danger. Harry had no claims on being a hero, far from it, but he also wasn't callous enough to watch a woman get injured, not if he could stop it.

"Go away."

Harry halted, then blinked. The little imposter—she barely reached his shoulder—had hissed at him out of the corner of her mouth. How had she known he was behind her? He hadn't made a single sound!

The two men looked up. They were cocky and obnoxious young men, overly confident because they'd been running their scam in this area for far too long, at least that's what Harry's friend, Dalton, had said. He owed Dalton, and stopping these ruffians from their petty extortion would be adequate compensation, but it was a nuisance. Especially if some stray with a weird agenda was determined to interfere and complicate matters.

One of the men turned to face them, propping his elbows on the counter and giving them both an assessing look. "What are you doing?"

Harry pretended not to understand. He stared at a shelf filled with canned goods, finally selecting some potted meat. He shuddered. Nasty looking stuff, potted meat. The little female remained frozen beside him.

After an extended silence where no one seemed willing to move, Harry looked up. "Hmm? You were talking to me?"

The guy pushed off the counter and started forward through the narrow, crammed aisles. His blond hair was long and greasy, like the rest of his body, and his eyes were a pale, washed-out blue, red-rimmed and with lashes so light they were nearly invisible. Scraggly whiskers dotted his chin, a discredit to every manly beard ever grown. His partner, heavier and darker, also turned to watch while the proprietor, a man close to seventy, seemed to grow more agitated by the moment.

"Yeah, you. Who did you think I was talking to? The kid?"

Harry smiled. So the guy was a dolt, believing she was a man. Or rather a boy. Was he myopic? Couldn't he *smell* her, for God's sake? Harry cocked an imperious brow. "I didn't hear the question."

Irritation flashed on blondie's face as he struck an insolent pose, one hip thrust out, his arms crossed on his narrow chest. "I asked what the hell you're doing."

Bells jingled as a customer started in, then jingled again as the woman took in the situation in a glance and hurried back out. Obviously the denizens of this area were well aware of what went on. They were all simply too old or too wary to stop it on their own. Harry wasn't old or wary. He stared down at the man with utter disdain.

"I'm shopping. What concern is it of yours?"

Blondie's face darkened and he straightened slightly. "You've been hanging around since we got here. Why haven't you bought anything yet?"

Harry raised both brows. Pushy little bastard. "I'm selective."

The young man scowled, his pale eyes going even

paler, then he obviously decided not to pursue it, probably given the fact that Harry stood a good six foot five, nearly half a foot taller than him. Though Harry dressed like a gentleman, few people ever thought of him as one. It was something, they said, to do with his eyes, though he tended to disregard such nonsense.

"Well, get done and get out. I don't like you hanging around."

Harry was willing to play along—up to a point. Right up until the punk turned to the girl and poked her in the chest with his finger, almost knocking her over. "Same goes for you. Beat it."

Harry wasn't a hero, he truly wasn't, but he detested bullies. Beyond that, he couldn't tolerate violence of any kind toward females, regardless of the fact the fellow was too dense to realize she *was* a female.

When he started to add an additional poke, snickering at the way she'd stumbled, Harry dropped the potted meat—no big loss there—and snatched the fellow's finger into his fist. Harry squeezed.

A loud wail of outraged pain filled the store.

Unconcerned, Harry asked, "Now, why would you want to inflict abuse on someone smaller than yourself?"

The guy's knees were starting to give way as Harry ruthlessly tightened his grip. Blondie stared up at him, his face pinched in a grimace. "He's almost as tall as I am!"

"Not an adequate excuse. You're obviously older. And moreover, I've decided I don't like you." Using a deft movement of his own hand, Harry twisted the hapless finger, attached to an equally hapless arm, until the man was forced to go on tiptoe, high-pitched curses winging from his mouth.

Pandemonium broke out.

The little female overflowed with umbrage. "I don't need your help, you pompous ass!" The men either ignored her, or didn't hear her.

The bully's dark friend rushed forward. "Floyd!" he called out, as he pulled a gun from his pants. His gaze lifted to Harry, narrow-eyed and mean. "Turn him loose before I shoot your head off!"

The hard nose of a gun barrel poked into Harry's ribs. He cast a wry expression on the friend. "Now, that'd be rather difficult, with you aiming there. My head's a bit higher up."

His ill-advised insult got the gun immediately raised, and now he felt the cold metal against his ear. This comedy of errors was getting out of hand. Slowly, he loosened his grip.

Floyd shook his hand and cursed, then shook it some more. He looked up at Harry with red-rimmed eyes. "Shoot him."

"What?"

"Damn it, you heard me, Ralph! *Shoot him.*"

Harry said a quick prayer. The girl, finally showing some small signs of intelligence, began inching her way nonchalantly toward the door.

"Get back here, damn it." Floyd wasn't about to let her, or rather him, get away. "I think you two are working together to distract us. Who sent you here?"

The little female blinked and her smooth cheeks

were suffused with color. "No one sent me! And I never saw that guy before in my life."

Harry waited for a gasp, waited for the recognition because her husky voice had obviously been that of a female's, despite her efforts to lower it accordingly.

He waited in vain.

"We can't jus' shoot him, Floyd. You know what Carlyle said. Keep it tidy. Besides, it'll be easier if we jus' let him go. He's nobody."

"Then what was he buttin' his nose in for?"

Ralph lowered his brows in thought, all the while keeping the gun steady on Harry's head.

Trying to placate them, Harry shrugged and said, "I simply can't abide a bully."

The gun smacked against his head, making his ears ring. "You can *abide* anythin' Floyd tells you to! That's how it's done in these parts."

Floyd grinned, and Harry was amazed to see he had fairly even, white teeth. "So you didn't like me pushing the scrawny runt around?"

Knowing he'd handed Floyd his revenge on a silver platter, Harry almost groaned. Damn his mouth anyway. He started to speak, his brain searching for words to defuse the situation, and in that instant Floyd backhanded the woman. She went sprawling, landing with a clatter in a stacked display of canned tuna.

Harry growled, discretion forgotten, and lunged forward to grab Floyd by the neck. The proprietor shouted. Ralph, the only one thinking at this point, snatched the woman up and held the gun on her.

"Stop now or the little bastard's gonna be in some serious trouble."

Harry stopped. The woman was dazed, he could see that, a bruise already coloring her jaw, but she was otherwise unharmed. Breathing hard with his anger, Harry slowly opened his hand and Floyd stumbled back two steps—and threw a punch. Harry caught the fist an inch from his nose, then made "tsking" sounds of disapproval. "I do believe your associate said to stop."

"He was talking to you, not me!"

Harry heaved an annoyed sigh. "Look, gentlemen, you obviously had business here and it's gotten sidetracked. Perhaps you should let us innocent bystanders go and finish up whatever it was you started?" Rather than observing, as he'd wished, Harry had managed to complicate things hideously. Now he only hoped to salvage what he could.

The proprietor nodded his head in frantic, disgruntled agreement. His low, scratchy voice was that of an aged sailor, used to taking command. "Yeah, take the damn cash. But put the gun away."

"Shut up, old man, and let me think."

Harry considered that an unlikely prospect given that Floyd obviously had very little brain to work with, but he held his peace. He didn't want to rile anyone further, especially the proprietor who looked ready for violence. That would be all he'd need to tip the scales into the never-imagined.

After a considerable amount of time, Floyd nodded. "I think you're a cop."

That straightened his spine. Harry blustered. "Don't be ridiculous."

A low whistle slipped past Ralph's drooping mustache. "Now that you say it, Floyd, he does look like a cop. Check out that coat he's wearing."

Rolling his eyes, Harry said, "You've been watching too much *Columbo*. It's drizzling today, therefore I wore a trench coat. I hardly think it's standard dress for the police force."

"Come to that," Ralph added, "you speak damn fancy for someone from these parts."

"I'm not from these parts."

Floyd jutted his chin forward. "Then what are you doing here?"

"I was in the area on business and I remembered I needed to pick up something for my dinner. It's no more complicated than that, I assure you."

"I don't believe you."

Well, hell, Harry thought, eyeing the female who now remained blessedly silent, her eyes downcast. Was he to be done in by a damn coat?

"Just to be on the safe side," Floyd said, grinning, "I think we'll take the boy with us. You call the cops, or try to follow, and I'll kill him."

The situation had gotten completely out of hand. "No, you can't do that."

Ralph tilted his head, his smile taunting. "And why not?"

The woman began to struggle. "I'm not going anywhere with you two! If you want a hostage, take him!" Her slender finger pointed in Harry's direction, disconcerting him for just a moment.

"Somehow I think you'll be easier to handle."

She kicked at Ralph's shin and he neatly side-stepped her, but Harry could see he was nonplussed by her somewhat feminine, awkward reaction. "What the hell?"

She tried to run. Harry was helpless, seeing the gun held steady, knowing any move on his part could get her injured. He wanted to curse at her theatrics, since she only complicated things further.

Floyd made a grab for her, and after his arms circled her chest, he too stopped, stunned. He released her as if burned, his eyes wide, going over her entire body in a single sweep.

"Take off your jacket."

"Go to hell!"

Floyd began to laugh. "I'll be a son of a... He's not a boy at all."

Dryly, for he was tired of the whole thing, Harry muttered, "How very astute of you."

Floyd swung around to glare at Harry, his voice a sneer. "I suppose you knew?"

"Of course."

Ralph drew a deep breath. "I don't like you much, mister."

The woman crossed her arms over her chest. "I don't like him at all."

Of all the nerve! Here he was, trying to preserve her ungrateful slender neck, and she—

"I said take off your jacket. Now. I want to get a better look at you."

Ralph held the gun pointed at her chest while Floyd

did his ordering. Gently, buying some time, Harry said, "Better do as they ask."

She glared at him. "Go to hell."

Trying to be reasonable, Harry said, "There you have it, gentlemen. Surely you can see you're wasting your time."

The elderly owner, fairly bristling in outrage, slapped an envelope down on the countertop, offering it like a bribe. "Here's your damn money. Forget the girl and get the hell out of my store!"

"Be quiet, Pops. Now, even if you don't take off the jacket, I won't shoot you. That'd be too messy and would probably ruin the fun of this. And Ralph and I do like a little fun every now and again, don't we Ralph?"

Ralph snickered.

"But if you don't take the damn thing off, and right now, I'll have Ralph shoot *him*."

The gun dutifully switched so once again it pointed at Harry.

After the briefest of hesitations, the girl shrugged, her chin elevated. "Go ahead, shoot him. What's it to me?"

Harry's chin hit his chest. Why that miserable little... "Now, see here!"

Enjoying himself, Floyd laughed. "So maybe you two aren't working together after all. It doesn't change anything. I want to see what you have under there, girlie. What are you hiding?"

She seemed to calm, and her eyes, which Harry just noticed were a very deep, dark blue rimmed with thick lashes, held steady. "Touch me and I'll kill you."

Both men laughed at that. Even Harry felt a small grin. The girl was so tiny, she couldn't hurt anyone, yet she had her fair share of bravado. He shifted, moving a little closer to the front window. No one noticed.

"Maybe I'll just have you get naked."

The owner was outraged. "You'll do no such thing! I have customers who come in regularly this late. It's not a quiet time. You need to take the money and—"

"*I told you to shut up.*"

Harry moved another few inches toward the window. Between the girl and the store owner, things were far too unpredictable. Was he the only one to realize how grave this situation had become? If he could just get in view and signal Dalton that things had gone wrong, they'd have backup in a matter of moments. Dalton's jewelry store sat directly across the street and was likely next on Floyd's list of stops.

He could see Floyd getting agitated, and besides being stupid and a bully, Floyd could well be trigger-happy. Harry didn't consider it wise to push him too far.

To distract the men from his subtle movements toward the window, he suggested, "You don't want my death plaguing your conscience, sweetheart. Remove the jacket. You can't have anything all that singularly special to hide."

"Huh?"

Floyd wasn't as confused as Ralph. "Yeah, it ain't like all of us men here, even Pops, haven't seen a woman naked before. And I really will have Ralph shoot him. Hell, I'm looking for a reason."

Her brows beetled down and her eyes narrowed. "It's no skin off my nose what you do with him."

At that moment Ralph looked out the window and cursed, then cursed again. "There's a couple of cops over at the jewelry store."

He was distracted for that moment, and Harry started forward, only to be brought up short as Ralph swung around, the gun moving wildly in his hand from Pops to the girl to Harry. "What do we do now, Floyd?"

But Floyd was already moving, snatching the envelope from Pops with a muttered warning, then pulling his own gun. He pointed it at Harry. "Out the back. You're coming with us."

Harry's first thought was, *Thank God, they're taking me instead of the girl.* Not that he was a hero, but he was trained for this, knew how to handle it. But then Floyd grabbed her, too.

Harry's muscles tightened all the way down to his toes. "Stop and think, Floyd. You don't need her. She'll just slow you down."

"If she tries that, she'll be sorry." And he sounded deadly serious, all fun and games over.

"One hostage is more than adequate."

"Be quiet, damn it. I've heard all I want to hear from you. Now move."

With guns at their backs, Harry and the girl were forced to exit out the rear of the store. Was Dalton still waiting for a signal? He wouldn't get one, not now. But why were the police there? Had Dalton somehow known things had gone wrong even without Harry's signal?

There were no answers to be found, and no more time to consider the circumstances as they were led through a light rain to a rental truck left parked in the dark alley. The sun was all but gone, and the mid-June air felt cool and thick. Floyd waved his gun, directing them into the open back of the truck. After hopping in, Harry turned to assist the woman, but she scrambled awkwardly in on her own, disdainfully ignoring his hand.

"You drive, Ralph. I'll ride in here with the little lady." His grin was more of a leer. "You two, into the corner. Sit and keep your mouths shut."

Harry took off his long trench coat and gallantly spread it over the dusty bottom of the empty truck floor, then signaled for the woman to sit. She gave him a furious look and perversely retreated into an opposite corner, slumping down and wrapping her arms around her bent legs. Her position pulled the jean material tight around her thighs and he could see she was slender, her bottom rounded. He forced his gaze to her face.

She looked dejected and in deep thought, but not, thankfully, as frightened as she should be. Her cheek was dark and swollen where she'd been hit, spurring his anger. Harry carefully lowered himself, keeping his eyes alternately on Floyd and the woman.

He hadn't counted on such a predicament when he'd agreed to take care of things for Dalton. He certainly hadn't counted on his attention being diverted by a woman. Any woman, but much less one who was trying to be a man and had an attitude problem. Out of all the female types in the world, headstrong, bossy, controlling women were his very least favorite. He'd had his fill of them long ago.

Yet he couldn't seem to keep his eyes off her.

Dim illumination filled the back of the truck as a small, battery-operated light came on. Ralph pulled the door down from the outside, sealing the three of them in. Harry knew he had to adjust his plans. He couldn't risk the possibility of being taken among the conspirators. The odds wouldn't be good and now he had an outsider to think about.

He eyed the woman again. Why was she involved? He didn't doubt for a moment that she'd been up to something, but his brain couldn't dredge up a single plausible motivation. She hadn't been aware of what she'd blundered into until it was too late, of that he was certain.

Floyd paced the back of the truck, agitated, for a good fifteen minutes while the truck raced farther and farther away from the police. No sirens sounded in the distance; there was nothing but the gentle patter of the rain and the grinding of the shifting truck gears.

"Sit together," Floyd said as he slid down the opposite wall and propped the gun on a knee. "I want to be able to keep you both in my sights."

Harry merely raised a brow at the woman and with a muttered oath, she stood and came to him, then plopped back down. "Bastard," she whispered.

Taken aback, Harry said aloud, and with a good deal of annoyance, "I beg your pardon?"

Suddenly she turned and slugged him in the arm. "This is all your fault! They were paying me no mind until you drew their attention to me."

He rubbed his arm where she'd socked him, more out of indignation than actual hurt, as he eyed her furious expression. "How was I to know Floyd and Ralph were too ignorant to recognize a woman when she presented herself?" Unaccountable female hysterics. He knew he was frowning at her, knew his frown was enough to frighten most grown men, and didn't care one whit. If he scared her, it served her right.

She slugged him again. "I was disguised, you fool!"

He caught her fist and held it, careful not to hurt her, then leaned so close their noses almost touched. Through clenched teeth, he growled, "Obviously not well enough since I picked you out right away."

He heard her swallow. Her eyes shifted on his face, nearly crossing, then finally narrowed in suspicion. "How?"

Knowing he held Floyd's fascinated attention, Harry saw no reason not to explain. In fact, he relished the moment. "Actually, you have a woman's mouth."

He looked at her mouth again—now set in a mulish line—and felt his stomach muscles tighten. He swallowed. *Damn her*. His gaze came back up to hers and stayed there. "You have a woman's bottom," he said with a taunting smile, "despite the baggy jeans. You also move like a woman."

He grinned, pulling her slightly toward him, primed for his last tribute. "And you smell very much like a woman."

The hit was direct; she stiffened and sputtered. "Don't be stupid! I'm not wearing perfume."

He searched her face, amazed by his own reaction. He answered softly. "I know."

Floyd laughed, once again showing his perfect white teeth. "I hadn't looked at her butt." He shrugged. "I thought she was a guy."

Effectively distracted, Harry blinked and moved a little away from her, but maintained his grip on her punching arm. "Yes, well, she afforded me an unimpeded view. And since I'm a...*healthy* male, and I noticed, I knew she had to be female."

"Warped male logic," she accused with excessive heat, and tried to jerk her hand away. He held firm. "So why did you have to make my sex known to the other two idiots?"

"Careful." Floyd was no longer amused.

"That was unintentional." When she huffed, he added, "I was trying to protect you, you ungrateful child."

"I'm not a child."

"How old are you?" Floyd asked. It amazed Harry that Floyd could be so easily diverted.

"None of your damn business!"

The rain began to come down in earnest, sounding like gunshots on the roof of the truck. Gears shifted, throwing Harry slightly off-balance and completely toppling the girl.

Floyd stretched out his legs to brace himself. "I'd say you're young, but not too young." He frowned in consideration. "No one's following us and we have a ways to go yet. Maybe you should just get naked now so I can judge for myself. You look a little too flat for my tastes, but you never know."

The truck shifted again and they were all three caught scrambling for balance. Floyd crudely cursed

Ralph's driving abilities. The woman landed on her hands and knees and, looking comparable to a rabid dog, she shouted, "For the last time you miserable worm, I am *not* taking anything off!"

Harry silently applauded her bravado, misplaced as it seemed.

Judging by the incredulous look on Floyd's face, he wouldn't be patient much longer, and with each mile that passed, their odds of getting out of this unscathed decreased.

They rode steadily uphill. From what Harry could tell they were heading out into the farming area. No residential homes there, and people would be scarce. He had to do something before they covered too much ground.

Harry got an idea. Risky, but he had to make an effort.

He bent a stern look on the woman and demanded, "Why not? For heaven's sake, your bosom can't be so spectacular that it's worth my life. Don't think I've forgotten you were willing to see me die to protect your dubious modesty."

She looked surprised, frozen, for only a heartbeat. Slowly, she turned to face him, her back to Floyd, her hands on her hips. Then to his shock, she gave him a wink, no smile, just that understanding wink that nearly floored him. At the same time she yelled, "I should have known you weren't really a hero! You're as bad as the other two."

He almost grinned. He did surge to his feet to tower over her. "Almost as bad? I'll have you know they're babies compared to me."

Floyd sputtered, no longer enjoying their show.

The woman leaped at him, the truck veered sharply left and they went down in a welter of arms and legs. Floyd yelled for them to stop, but they paid no heed. Their bodies rolled toward Floyd, twisting and fighting.

Harry made feigned attempts to subdue her while she did her best to bludgeon him with fists and feet. He caught himself alternately chuckling and struggling to keep from getting his nose broken. A sharp elbow in the ribs made him grunt.

Finally, finally Floyd got within reach, determined to end their scuffle. The woman neatly tripped him, and as he stumbled Harry snatched his gun hand and raised it to the roof, then clipped him hard in the chin.

He had very large, solid fists and Floyd went down without a whimper.

Breathing hard, the woman turned to him, stuck out her hand and said, "Thanks. I was starting to worry. My name's Charlie."

Harry laughed. "Charlie? I suppose that fits as well as anything else. You may call me Harry." He took her hand, noticing how slim and warm her fingers felt, then asked, "I didn't hurt you, did I?"

She snorted rudely as her eyes darted around the truck. "I say we toss his sorry butt out the back. I have things to do and they don't include going...wherever the hell it is we're going. Plus I have no desire to meet their pal, Carlyle."

Harry studied her, again stupefied. "You're not at all upset? You weren't frightened?"

"'Course I was."

She didn't look frightened. She looked determined to drag poor Floyd's body to the edge of the truck bed so she could throw him out. Never mind that it would probably kill him. Wasn't she squeamish about such a thing?

"Don't just stand there, give me a hand here. He's heavy."

Nope, not squeamish. Damn vicious female.

She could at least pretend *some* feminine qualities. He *really* didn't like bossy, overbearing women. Harry crossed his arms over his chest and studied her. "I'm sorry to disappoint you, miss, since you do seem rather set on your course, but I'm not up to killing a man."

"Coward." She heaved and pushed and dragged the body closer to the edge. "Besides, who says he'll die?"

"Now listen here—"

She jerked upright, her face flushed, one thick wisp of glossy black hair now hanging over her right eye. "No, you listen! You got me involved in this with your damn nosiness and misplaced heroism. This is all your fault. The very least you can do is...is..." Her voice dropped off and she covered her face with her hands. Her shoulders shook.

Harry had the horrible suspicion she might be crying.

Good God. He hadn't wanted her to be *that* female.

2

"DON'T YOU touch me." Charlie stared at the behemoth coming toward her, his expression now bemused. She drew a deep breath, absolutely refusing to give in to her tears, her disappointment. She felt humiliated and decided most of it was his fault. She lifted her chin in the air and said with disdain, "You've done plenty, already."

He held up his hands—very large, capable hands. "I'm sorry. But we don't have time for this." She started to speak, but then he put the gun in the back of his belt, and she wanted that gun, damn him. She didn't trust him, didn't trust anyone at this point, and needed to be able to protect herself. Whoever would have thought a simple Monday could get so dastardly confused?

After all her efforts to move Floyd—and she really did want to toss his body out—it took Harry only a second to heave him to the other end of the truck bed, well out of danger from falling out.

He pulled a knife from his own pocket, stripped off Floyd's jacket, and proceeded to cut it up. He used the cloth strips to tie and gag Floyd in record time.

"Now." He stood and dusted off his hands.

He seemed to have things well in control and that annoyed her anew. At first, he'd seemed too pretentious to get involved in a scuffle. But once he'd gotten involved, he'd been beyond impressive. It wasn't what she'd expected of him at all.

She was used to being the one in control, the one people came to for help. This man acted as though getting kidnapped and held at gunpoint was a regular part of his workweek. "Now what?"

The truck shifted again and Harry braced himself before giving her a wary, probing look. "You're not going to cry?"

"No." Charlie almost laughed at his look of relief. She hadn't figured him to be the type to fall apart over female tears. She gave him a sideways look. "How about you?"

He paused, stared at her a moment, then raised his brows. "I'm holding up. Completely dry-eyed."

"Good, because I can't stand blubbering men."

He gave her a small smile—a very charming smile actually, and she was beyond shocked that she noticed. She ducked her chin to avoid looking at him.

"We're on an incline," he noted thoughtfully. He picked up his coat from the corner, shook it out, then slipped it back on. "Let me get the door open and see where we're headed."

Charlie bit her lip and mustered up a calm tone. Nothing ventured, nothing gained, she'd always heard. "Since you have the knife, I'll hold the gun."

"No."

She bristled at his blunt reply. "Why not?"

Harry carefully lifted the door a foot or so, then laid on his belly and peeked out. He kept looking at her over his shoulder, as if he expected her to push him out as she'd planned to do with Floyd. It wasn't a bad idea, except that it'd be impossible; he was twice as big as Floyd and very alert. Besides, she didn't particularly want to get that close to him.

His thick brown hair dripped with rain when he pulled his head back inside. "We're near the Wayneswood exit."

Charlie gasped. "Wayneswood!" She hadn't realized they'd traveled quite so far. Her heart started an erratic pounding. "I have to get home."

"Come here." Harry lifted the door a bit more and sat, hanging his legs over the edge. He took the time to overlap his long coat, protecting his trousers as much as possible from the pounding rain.

Once Charlie had settled beside him—accepting whatever his plan might be, because she had none of her own—Harry took her hand. She jerked and had to struggle not to pull away. She didn't want to look like a wilting ninny.

"As the truck travels uphill," Harry explained, "it will have to slow down even more. We can jump out then. Luckily the rain will help conceal us, in the event Ralph glances out his mirror."

"It's too dark for him to see us."

"Perhaps. But a flash of movement might draw his attention and we can't take the chance. So lie low as soon as you can. Just flatten out on the road and we'll hope the truck keeps going. I don't relish the idea of getting into a shoot-out."

"Coward. Give me the gun."

He grinned and shook his head at her. "Valiant try,

but I don't provoke that easily, so you can hold the insults."

He completely ignored the rude sound she made.

"Besides, I have experience in handling guns."

His large hand felt so warm, and his muscled thigh pressed hard against her own. She shivered. Handholding with an appealing man was definitely not on the agenda for today. For the most part, it hadn't been on the agenda for her entire life. Raising her free hand, she flicked her earring with the flattened bullet attached. "So do I."

"You mean that trinket is real? And here I thought it was part of your costume."

She ground her teeth. He was humoring her, and she wouldn't put up with it. "It's real."

"Hmm." She was very aware of his thumb rubbing along her knuckles, and his close scrutiny. "Whatever could you possibly be involved in that would require a gun?"

To ease her own tension, and diffuse his attentions, she said, "I own a bar. Usually it's as dull as dishwater, but one night things got too rowdy and there was gunfire. This particular bullet missed my head by an inch. I decided it was lucky. You?"

He watched her too closely and far too long before he answered. With an elegant shrug he said, "I'm a private investigator." And that was that.

With no more confidences forthcoming, Charlie turned her attention back to the weather. "We're going to be drenched." Already her jeans were wet at the bottom. Her legs didn't extend nearly as far as his, but the rain blew furiously in all directions.

"True enough. However, it's not all that cold yet and the rain helps to mask the noise we make in the truck. I'm grateful to Mother Nature for her assistance."

Charlie made a face at him, though he didn't see it. So calm, so sure of what he planned to do. She wanted to know what was going on, who he was and what he'd been up to, why Floyd and Ralph had taken money from the store owner and what a private investigator had to do with it. Her curiosity was pricked, even though she had no room for other mysteries, other ventures. And now definitely wasn't the time. First she had to get back to Corsville. All her plans, shot through.

"You'd truly have let them shoot me?"

She lifted her face to see Harry studying her. He was so sure of himself, so arrogant. *So damn good-looking.* "Of course," she lied, disconcerted with his stare and just annoyed enough to goad him. She evidently used enough sincerity because his fierce frown reappeared.

Despite his obvious polish, he looked almost demonic with that evil glare. His incredible light brown eyes seemed scorching hot and far too probing, as if he could see inside her. She shivered, then shook off the fanciful thoughts. He was just a man like all the others, bigger, definitely stronger and more eloquent, but still fairly basic and ruled by simple motivations. She could, and would, control him.

His gaze lowered to her chest. "I can't imagine why. You don't appear to have anything all that spectacular to conceal."

He was going for the jugular, but Charlie, having worked in a bar for the past seven years, wasn't even tempted by the familiar baiting. At least her disguise had worked well. She was wearing enough layers to keep her warm and conceal any feminine curves at the same time.

Harry squeezed her hand to regain her attention and his expression was still too intent. "It's not that I haven't been shot before, you understand, but—"

"You should be more careful with your gun."

His eyes darkened, grew hotter. "Not with *my* gun, you little—"

"Listen. Isn't he shifting now? And if I'm not mistaken, the truck is slowing."

Harry gave her a long look of promised retribution. "Yes." He pulled his long legs up against the bed of the truck, bracing himself. "Time for us to go."

Charlie gulped. She looked down at the passing roadway beneath her and winced. True enough the truck had slowed, but the road still flew by them.

"One..."

"Ah, maybe—"

"Two..."

"Wait a second!"

"...three."

"*Harry!*"

"Go." And with that, he gave her a shove while using his muscular bulk to propel them out. They landed together, their hands still linked, and somehow Harry managed to get beneath her so that he cushioned much of her fall, not that his hard body felt much more giving than the roadway. They tumbled before coming to a dead stop, her on top, their legs tangled together. But just as quickly he rolled to the left, putting her beneath him—and into a very large icy puddle. She sucked in her breath with the shock of it.

His enormous body covered her completely, unmoving, heavy and hard. For the moment she was unable to think with any clarity. It felt as though her teeth had been jarred loose and with his great hulking weight on her, she couldn't draw a deep breath. Rain struck her face, icy cold and stinging against her flesh.

After a moment he lifted his head and looked behind them. Rain ran in rivulets from his hair to her chest. "The truck lights are going around the bend. I do believe Ralph is totally unaware that he's lost his guests."

When she didn't respond, he looked down at her. Charlie stared at his shadowed features in the darkness, struck again by his perfect handsomeness. He seemed such a contradiction. A fancy-pants, but with a lumberjack's body. A gallant hero, but still a bit earthy. She couldn't help but be awed by him, and she hated it.

His head lowered until he blocked the worst of the rain from her face, until she could feel the warmth of his breath on her lips. Her chest constricted the tiniest bit more.

It was absurd! She'd long ago learned the truth about men and their deceptions. But now, at the most unlikely of times, her mind had gone wandering along wayward paths.

Still, she could feel him from breasts to knees, and

he was firm and muscled and *big*. The wet ground and the danger seemed to fade for just a moment.

"Are you all right?"

His voice was low and deep and she wondered at it, even as she felt her belly curl in response to his tone. "I can't breathe."

His gaze dropped to her mouth and lingered for long moments. He closed his eyes and turned his head away. "My apologies." Gingerly, he removed himself, groaning every so often. He offered her a hand and together they sat there in the middle of the road. "I lingered in the hopes of feeling something worthy of my life, but you seem to be all pointy bones."

"What are you whining about?" As she stood, forcing her wobbly legs to support her, she squished. The puddle had seeped beneath her leather jacket to the layers of padding beneath. She was soggy as an old dishrag and probably holding about a gallon of water.

"Your breasts, sweetheart, those magnificent assets that are worth my life."

Oh for pity's sake. "Are you still harking on about that?" She looked around and saw nothing but darkness and endless stretching highway. The rain continued to fall, but luckily there was no traffic. None at all. "Where are we?"

"Yes, I'm still harking. It is my life, after all, though it obviously means little enough to you. And I'd say we're in the middle of the damn road, somewhere between Corsville and oblivion, getting more sodden by the second."

She started walking, leaving him behind. With every step, her boots, two sizes two large and now slick with the rain from the inside out, rubbed against her heels. It wasn't a pleasant feeling and she knew before long she'd have horrible blisters. But what else could she do? Stand around and wait for Ralph to return? Miss the grand performance she'd waited a lifetime to witness?

Probably, her thinking continued, she'd already missed it. That prospect angered her so much, she ignored Harry when he called to her.

"Hold up." His large hand closed on her arm and pulled her to a halt. "We can't just traipse down the middle of the road. In case it's escaped your notice, Floyd and Ralph are not nice men. They could double back looking for us. We need to get out of sight."

True enough, she thought, and nodded. "Yeah, and I suppose that means the woods." She glanced down at his dress shoes. "And with this downpour, it'll be a swamp." Her smile wasn't entirely nice. She started in that direction, and Harry followed. Both sides of the highway were lined with thick trees and little else.

"I can see by your snide expression you expect me to have a certain aversion to mud?"

She kept walking. "I hope not, 'cause big and heavy as you are, you'll sink up to your knees."

Harry turned up his collar and swiped the rain from his face, then shaded his eyes. "With all those trees acting as an umbrella, the ground might not be as saturated as you think."

"You hope."

He ignored her. "And likely the woods abut a farm or some sort of residential dwelling. We could get access to a phone."

She turned to face him. "All right, have you convinced yourself?"

His look of condescension had her grinning again. "I was attempting to reassure you, but I see the effort was wasted. Allow me to lead."

"Sure thing, Harry." At least his big body would block some of the rain. She stumbled along behind him in her heavy, soaked clothes, more miserable than she'd ever been in her life—not that she'd let him know it.

Harry took her arm. "You surprise me. I didn't expect you to be so agreeable."

She hunched both shoulders against the rain and trod onward, pulled along by his hand on her arm. "I'm easy."

His chuckle could be heard even over the rainstorm. "No grand confessions here, if you please. Not when I can't do anything about them."

She tried to stare at him, lost at his words, but he more or less dragged her behind him. "What's that supposed to mean?"

He grinned again; she couldn't see it, but she could hear it. "I appreciate an *easy* woman as much as the next man. But these conditions aren't exactly conducive to seduction."

Appalled, she forgot to watch her step and tripped over a tree root. Harry pulled her upright before her face hit the mud. *Of all the outrageous!*... "I wasn't talking about sex, you idiot!"

They continued a few more feet, and luckily, though the mud did suck at her too-big boots, it was drier, the rain not so blinding, filtered by the many trees.

"That's for the best, I suppose, since I don't as yet know what you have to offer. All I know is that you apparently think it's worth a man's life."

She rolled her eyes and decided to ignore him. Several minutes later, she was wincing in pain.

Harry stopped and turned to frown down on her. Without the rain lashing her face, her eyes were able to adjust to the darkness, and once again she found herself scrutinizing him.

He was by far the biggest man she'd ever seen, tall and thickly muscled, but with grace, if such a thing was possible. And he had the strangest eyes, a shade lighter than his medium brown hair, almost a whiskey color, but bright and thick lashed. Intense, bordering on wicked. When he looked at her, she actually felt it; she'd felt it even back in the store. That's how she'd known he was creeping up on her, intent on telling her something. She hadn't wanted his attention or anyone else's. She'd wanted to be able to concentrate on her first small victory in her private war.

But the plan had fallen through. Damn Dalton Jones.

Harry touched her chin, his fingers gentle. "What's the matter? I expected a tenacious little mug like you to keep up, not lag behind."

She sighed. Showing a weakness to this man, any weakness, went against the grain. He was the one out of his element, yet he hadn't offered a single complaint. But there was no hope for it. "My feet are killing me."

"Ah, I see. Well, since I may want to retain that pleasure for myself—killing you, that is—why don't you explain to me exactly what the problem is?"

The threat didn't alarm her. She was already used to his wry sense of humor and didn't fear him at all. "My boots are too big and now that they're wet they're sliding up and down and I can feel the blisters on my heels. It hurts."

He stared down at her, those eyes of his bright in the darkness, like a wild animal surveying prey, making her shiver with a strange and exciting feeling. But his voice, in comparison, was soft, inquiring. "Why are your boots too large?"

She scowled, attempting to ignore the fluttering in her stomach. "Because I hadn't exactly planned on trudging through the woods in them."

Coming down on his haunches in front of her, he said, "Give me your foot."

"The bottom is covered in mud."

"I'll survive."

He lifted her foot and wiggled her boot, judging the size while ignoring her cry of pain—the jerk.

"I have some knit gloves in my pocket. Do you think you could stuff them into the heels as a little padding?"

Her sore feet loved the idea. "Yeah, thanks."

To her surprise, he picked her up.

To her further surprise, he cursed and hastily set her back down again when streams of rainwater squished out of her clothing to run down his chest. "What in the world are you wearing? You feel like a sodden mop and weigh a ton."

She flushed, both from his initiated gallantry and

his censure. She wasn't used to either. No man tried to schmooze her, and they sure as hell didn't try to boss her around. Through gritted teeth, she explained, "I have a few...layers on."

Though she tried to duck away, one large hand reached beneath her jacket and clutched at the material over her rib cage. He squeezed, and it was like wringing out a rag. "Ah. I assume this is why your precious breasts are invisible?"

Overcome with embarrassment, ready to drown him in the nearest available mud puddle, she nodded. "And you can shut your mouth on any more questions because it's none of your damn business anyway!"

"My curiosity grows in leaps and bounds."

"I hope you choke on your blasted curiosity."

He laughed. "Come on, and no, I won't carry you regardless of how your feet hurt."

"I wasn't going to ask!"

He assisted her to a fallen log amidst tons of greenery. Charlie prayed it wasn't poison ivy vines twining everywhere. Harry crouched in front of her again and tugged off the boots.

"I'm sorry. I know it hurts." He pulled the gloves from his pockets, folded one in half and put it inside her sock. "Let's try this and see how it works." After both feet were repaired and her boots back on, she stood.

"How does it feel?"

The gloves were soft and thankfully dry. She took a few careful steps, then smiled. "Much better. Thanks. You're a handy man to have around, Harry."

He opened his mouth and she said, "If ever again I find myself kidnapped and then abandoned in a rainstorm on an empty highway bordering the woods while wearing boots that are too big, why then, you're just the man I'd want to..."

A beep sounded, interrupting her teasing, and they both jumped. Harry started to shove her behind him and she laughed. "I appreciate your efforts to save me from my pager, but I think I can handle it."

He muttered a low curse.

Charlie looked at the lit dial and added her own, more heated and descriptive curses to his.

He tsked her language, then asked, "An important call?"

"My sister."

"Will she worry about you and send someone to find you? Did she know where you were today?"

"Yes and no and no."

"I forgot the order of my questions. Care to clarify?"

Charlie felt like crying. Her poor sister. She hadn't wanted Charlie to go through with her scheme. She'd said it didn't matter. And now she'd be sick with worry.

"Charlie?"

It was the first time he'd called her by name and she liked the way his cultured tones made it sound. Everyone she knew called her Charlotte, despite her protestations. Her mother had set the example, and everyone had followed it. Except for her sister, but then her sister loved her.

"I hate to say it, Harry, but no, no one will look for

us. My sister will worry when I don't call her back, but she won't know what to do, or where to check."

She fell silent for a long time, her thoughts dark and troubled, when Harry touched her arm. "Are you all right?"

That particular tone was new coming from him, and it surprised her. No one worried about her. "Of course."

"You're quiet and I don't like it." His hand touched her cheek, her ear. "I don't want you to turn too brooding on me. It unnerves me and won't help anything."

"So distract me."

She saw the flash of his grin before he tried to hide it. "I'd be glad to oblige you, even though you're too short and your assets are still rather questionable, regardless of the high value you've put upon them—"

"Harry."

"—but again, it's just too messy out here. Too much mud and too many weeds I don't recognize and don't want my more private body parts to come into contact with. Plus, I don't know anything about you, why you're dressed as a male, if you're possibly gay—"

"I'm not gay."

"Well, being that we're alone for who knows how long, that's a comfort of sorts I suppose."

Charlie stopped. She turned to face him, her hands fisted. "Will you stop blathering on. And what possible difference could it make to you if I'm gay or not?"

"We may never find civilization again. Or at least, it could take more hours than I'm willing to ponder. Feminine company might come in handy. Think about it. It's almost romantic. All alone in a dark woods, silence all around us. Only my body to keep you warm and protect you."

Though she knew he was being sarcastic, her stomach tingled at his words. She could almost feel his heat.

Men *never* flirted with her, if indeed that's what he was doing. Men threw lewd comments her way on occasion, but she doubted Harry could sound lewd if he tried.

She dredged up her own sarcasm to mask her response. "All we need is candlelight and wine?"

His voice lowered to a sexy rumble. "I never imbibe when with a woman. It dulls the senses, you know, and I prefer to feel everything as it's supposed to be felt."

Despite herself, she drew in a long breath of surprise.

He laughed, then flicked her nose. "Also a flashlight is more economical. Candlelight is far too vague." He pulled a small penlight from his pocket, dangling with his keys from a key chain. "I think I'd like a nice sharp beam of light so I can fully explore things. Especially these mysterious breasts of yours." A skinny beam of light flashed over her shoulders and she jerked around, giving him her back. She saw the light coast lower.

"Harry," she warned.

"Hmm?"

"You're being outrageous." She started walking again, no better reply forthcoming.

"Thank you." When she snorted, he said, "I did manage to distract you, didn't I?"

She paused in her stride, but just for a moment. "I suppose. Now tell me why you were in that store, what a private investigator has to do with Floyd and Ralph. And, oh yeah, who's Carlyle?"

"If I tell will you tell?"

"Kind of like, show me yours and I'll show you mine?"

"I'm willing if you are. Of course, I don't have the added pressure of having to produce something worth a man's life."

Charlie laughed, she couldn't help herself. For several years now, she'd disdained men, her supposed father especially, though she didn't remember the man all that well anymore, the long ago memories and her mother's words mixing together in confusion. Today might have been the day to end the confusion, but everything had gone worse than wrong.

As to the others, the men who sat in her saloon night after night, drinking themselves into a stupor, claiming their wives were responsible or irresponsible or dull. And her mother's old boyfriends, no accounts without a future or the urge to motivate. They were all jerks and users and she had nothing but contempt for them all.

Harry was different. He was outrageous, true, but he made her laugh and his outrageousness wasn't a threat or an insult, but rather a game, a certain charming wit that he employed with skill. She had no fear he would force her, or that he'd actually try to humiliate her as Floyd had. He was big and brave, and something of a hero, a fact she couldn't deny since she'd seen herself the efforts he'd made to try to protect her, even with a gun to his head.

"How old are you, Harry?"

"An odd question, coming out of the blue like that, but why not? As a conversational gambit, it beats the obvious chitchat of weather, and it's as good as any other. I'm thirty-two. And you?"

"Are you a good private eye?"

"Meaning?"

"Do you make much money at it?"

He cleared his throat. "Less of a gambit, but yes, I support myself nicely if that's what you mean."

He was probably expensive, too expensive, but maybe she could figure something out. "How long have you been in the detecting business?"

"Detecting? Well, let's see. About six years now."

"Are you kind to animals?"

He laughed. "There's a purpose to this interview? All right, I'll trust there is. I have two dogs and a cat and they love me or at least they pretend to in order to get me to do their bidding or sometimes when I find a chewed up shoe or a mess in the corner. Does that answer your question?"

"Are you married?"

"Did you have an unemployed dog in mind that you're hoping to foist off on me?"

A small lump of dread formed in her stomach and she struggled to keep her tone light. "So you are married?"

"Divorced, actually, not that it should concern you."

She turned to face him. He was big and gorgeous and funny and a hero. He might well be the man she needed. God knew her level of success on her own hadn't been anything to boast about, especially given today's incredible fiasco. "I think I like you, Harry."

"Look there," Harry said, pointing over her head and studiously ignoring her last statement. "A building of some sort. I do believe salvation is at hand."

Charlie looked in the direction he indicated. They'd wandered completely through the woods to another road. A small block building, bludgeoned by the rain, sat close to the road, looking indeed like salvation.

Harry, his face averted, plodded onward and Charlie gladly let him lead the way, content to follow behind. To say she trusted him now would definitely be going too far, but he'd made her laugh and that was a huge accomplishment. As to the rest, she'd just have to wait and see.

3

"WELL WHAT DO you know, it's an abandoned gas station."

Harry stood in a spot of grease, thankfully out of the rain, and studied their little Eden. He'd had to kick in the door, which had proved remarkably easy given the rotting wood and rusty lock. Likely inhabited by any number of critters, it was still dry and safe and a block against the growing breeze. The rain finally began to taper off, but with that concession came a chill that sank bone-deep. The temperature had dropped by several degrees and he could see Charlie's lips shivering. Nice lips, sort of pouty in a seductive way, especially for a woman who wasn't all that attractive and seemed to have a problem with cordial behavior. Would she have really let them shoot him?

Damn her, he just didn't know.

"How long has it been empty do you think?"

She stood huddled in the middle of the floor, her arms wrapped tight around herself, her knees knocking together, determined not to utter a single complaint, as if admitting to the cold was a weakness. Strange woman.

A growing puddle formed around her. Her hair had mostly come loose from the rubber band and was starting to curl just the tiniest bit.

"Perhaps from the time they put in the highway some five years ago. This is the old county road. No one travels it anymore which is, I presume, the reason this particular station closed up."

"The road must still lead somewhere though, to a house or two."

"No doubt, but we won't be finding any help in this storm. You're the picture of misery, half-frozen and too tired to budge. Time to get as dry as possible." He looked at her, saw her staring back wide-eyed, and added, "That means removing your ridiculous costume."

She froze in the process of rubbing her arms, sluicing off more water. "Is that the only tune you know? All right, damn it, I lied. I wouldn't have let them shoot you, not if I could help it. But I knew if they thought I cared, they'd think we were together. I wanted them to take you and forget about me."

Well, that was brutal honesty of a sort. Not quite what he'd had in mind, but... "Believe it or not, Charlie, it was my wish as well." He found a crate, tested it for sturdiness and sat down with a deep groan of pleasure. "I had no desire to be responsible for you, and in fact I could have defused this entire situation if you hadn't screwed things up."

"*It was you—*"

He held up a hand. "No more bickering. And no more ridiculous modesty. Your belated concern for my safety has nothing to do with anything. I don't want to be lugging a half-dead woman back to town tomorrow, and that's what you'll be if you don't make some effort to warm yourself. It has nothing to do with my curiosity over your precious body parts."

"You have only my welfare in mind?"

"Quit sneering." He felt a smile tug at his lips and firmly repressed the urge to grin at her. "Come now, you must be in your mid-twenties at least. Surely you can't claim all that much modesty. I promise not to be impressed no matter what you unveil."

She looked ready to strike him, so he quickly added, "I'll make the grand sacrifice. My coat is still fairly dry on the inside, given that it's made for this weather and water repellent. You can wrap up in it after you've gotten out of your wet clothes."

She chewed her lips, thinking of heaven knew what, and finally shaking her head. More hair slipped free and clung to her forehead and cheeks. She didn't look like a boy now; she looked like a drowned rat. A wide-eyed, nervous rat. "No."

"What if I insist?"

She went stiff as a poker. "Insist all you want! I'm not taking anything off and I'm not—" Her voice dwindled into a very ratlike squeak when he started toward her. "Don't you dare touch me!"

"You're being unreasonable, Charlie. I hadn't thought you the type to submit to hysterics, but what else can it be? You can't be comfortable and if there was enough light to see, I have no doubt you'd be a pale shade of blue." He caught her arm and she tried to jerk away. He easily caught the neck of her jacket and stripped it off her, despite her efforts and the volume of her rank curses. The woman had the vocabulary of a sailor. "It's too dark in here for close observation anyway. What exactly do you suppose I'll see?"

"You'll see nothing because you're going to take your hands off me right now."

That calm tone of hers should have given him a warning, but he was too intent on forcing her to accept his benevolence. He was wet also, yet he'd offered her his coat, which would leave him with only his dress shirt and undershirt. Contrary to popular female opinion, men were not impervious to the cold. She should be thanking him, not cursing his ancestors. Why were women always so stubborn?

And then he felt the gun press into his ribs. He almost laughed. She'd done nothing but surprise him since he'd first spotted her. It was entertaining when it wasn't so annoying.

"Ah, you're fast. Don't tell me. You were a pickpocket once, weren't you, as well as a saloon girl? No, don't lie to me."

"I wasn't going to lie! I'm not a *saloon girl*, I'm the owner, and no, I was never a pickpocket. It's just that you weren't paying attention." She pressed the gun harder against him. "And you're *slow*."

In the next instant he jerked up her wrist and snatched the gun from her hand. In the process, it fired, the sound loud and obscene, sending particles of ceiling plaster to rain down on their heads. They both heard a flurry of scurrying from around them.

The shock left them still as statues. "Good grief, what was that?"

Harry was aware of her uneasiness, even her breath held. "Rats. And at the moment, they're the least of your worries." This time he stuck the gun a good distance inside his pants, then dared her with a look to try retrieving it. "Now."

She quickly regained her aplomb. "You're lucky you didn't shoot me!"

"I'd say you were luckier, being that you would have been the one shot." He took a firm step toward her.

"All right." She held up her hands. "Give me your coat, then turn your back and close your eyes."

"No." The silly woman persisted in her belief that he was an idiot.

"You're not going to watch, Harry."

"In case it's escaped your notice, it's exceedingly dim in here. What miserly moonlight there is can hardly penetrate the rain and the dust on the broken windows. I can't see my own hand in front of my face." That was an exaggeration; he could see just fine, but she didn't need to know that.

"I'll give you the coat, and if you'll promise not to do anything else foolish, I'll try to find a propitious spot for us to nest in until this storm completely blows over."

She curled her lip at him. "Your diction is astounding."

"Thank you." He handed her the coat and turned away, kicking debris with his feet as he carefully walked.

"It wasn't a compliment!" she called out, her voice heavy with sarcasm. "You're what the regulars at my bar would call a *fancy-pants*."

"I'm wounded to my soul by their censure." The

station stunk, literally. He could smell oil and rotting vegetation and heaven only knew what else. He preferred not to ponder the possibilities. He retrieved his tiny flashlight, flicked the light around in a wide arc, avoiding Charlie's dark corner, then settled on an area that would have to do.

"I've found a spot that's fairly dry and empty, and there's an old car bench seat. I suppose it'll support us and keep us off the cold cement floor."

He heard a "plop" and knew she'd dropped part of her disguise. He smiled in the darkness. "What exactly did you have on under your shirt?"

"Some old linen, pinned in place." Another plop. "Why don't you sit on the bench just to make sure nothing else is nesting there. I'm not keen on sharing with rats."

"I'm sure they feel the same about you." He kicked the seat with his foot. Nothing happened. Holding the flashlight in his teeth, he lifted one end and dropped it. And then did it again. "Nothing but an abundance of dust."

Another plop.

He turned off the flashlight before the temptation became too overwhelming. His eyeballs almost itched with the urge to peek. "Exactly how many layers did you have on?"

"Enough to get rid of any lumps or bumps, which was easy since my femaleness isn't all that noticeable anyway."

Temptation swelled. He looked toward her voice, but could only see a vague outline. He felt cheated and stared harder, but still only got shifting shadows and a stinging sense of guilt.

A wet length of toweling slapped up against his face. "You can use that to wipe off our nest."

Grumbling, he did as instructed then turned to her again. "I beg to differ. About your femaleness, I mean." He noticed her voice shook when she talked, more from cold now than anything else. His concern doubled. "If you'll recall, I knew right away that you were a female sort of person."

"I don't understand that. No one else noticed."

He could hear the chattering of her teeth. Definitely the cold. "Come here, Charlie. Let me warm you."

Not a sound. Not a movement. The irritating little twit.

"Oh for pity's sake." Though he tried to hide it, his irritation came through. "Charlie? Come on, I've proven myself by now, haven't I? We may have the entire night ahead of us, with nothing but the rain and the rats for company. Regardless of how stoic you might be, I don't mind admitting I'm cold. Let's at least make the attempt to get warm."

She took a step out of the shadows and he could see her vigorously rubbing her hair with her discarded shirt. His coat covered her from neck to ankles, enormously big on her petite frame. "What, exactly, did you have in mind?"

"A little cuddling." He smiled, already feeling the anticipation which was surely odd considering she really wasn't all that attractive and she had a penchant for insulting him with every breath. It was a unique feeling for him, being insulted by a woman. Even his ex-wife had refrained from that, at least until the very end. Before that, she'd been cajoling and sweet, even as she tried to manipulate him. Unaccountably, Charlie's bluntness piqued his interest. There was no understanding the workings of male hormones. "I'm willing to sacrifice myself by being on the bottom. You can sit on my, ah, lap and with our combined body heat we should stay warm enough."

"I don't know."

Her hair was a tousled dark mass of shining black, some locks hanging down to her eyes, other flipping around her ears. She looked almost cute, in a disheveled, bedraggled way. "Charlie, did you take everything off?" Now *his* voice shook. Damn it.

"No, of course not! My jeans are wet, but that can't be helped. I did remove those muddy boots, though, so you don't have to worry about them."

"My gratitude knows no bounds."

"What about you?"

He cleared his throat. "Just damp around the collar. Except for my pants, which are soaked."

"Leave them on."

He grinned again, but kept his tone mild. "I have no intention of lacerating your dubious sensibilities by strutting around naked. Now come here."

The stillness was palpable.

Harry sighed. "If you're hesitating because I said you smelled nice, well, keep in mind I feel the same about new leather and burnt sugar, but neither has ever inspired me to levels of uncontrollable lust."

He heard her grousing and mumbling, heard her shifting, then she moved a little closer. And damned if he didn't catch a whiff of her elusive scent again, now mixed with the dampness of the rain and the fresh outdoors. With his eyes closed, he breathed deeply.

"Why burnt sugar?"

She'd sidled close, near enough that he could see her clearly, could reach out and touch her. He did, his fingers first landing on her narrow shoulder, and when she didn't bolt, he let them slide down to her slender wrist. His coat sleeves had been rolled up but still hung down to her fingertips. She'd buttoned up all the way, but the coat was so big on her, the neckline hung disturbingly low. All in all, she looked adorable in his coat, all wet and stubborn and mulish. *Only, he didn't like stubborn, mulish women.*

He sat on the bench and tugged her down to his lap, giving her a moment to get used to the feel of that and giving himself a chance to calm his stampeding heart.

Ridiculous. There was absolutely no reason to react so strongly to her. She was just a woman, caught up in the same bizarre circumstances as he. Masculine interest hadn't prompted his offer to share body warmth. No, his motives were altruistic, they were—

"Harry?"

He could feel her breath on his throat when she spoke, feel her shivers. His awareness of her as a woman was acute. Slowly, wary of getting slugged at any moment, he wrapped his arms around her. "A friend of my father's used to make me this candy. He called it burnt sugar, and I suppose that's exactly what it is. He puts plain white sugar in a small buttered metal dish, melts it in the oven until the edges are dark brown, then lets it cool and harden. It's sort of like a sucker without the stick, and has a different taste since it isn't flavored at all. As a child, I forever had sticky fingers from eating burnt sugar."

She relaxed slightly, her body settling more closely into his and he could feel her heartbeat, could hear her breathing. "I can't imagine you as small, or with sticky fingers. You're so big now, and you seem so... fastidious."

"Yes, well, we all must grow up." Hoping to catch her off-guard, he asked, "What were you doing there, Charlie? And why the cross-dressing costume?"

She turned her face inward, doing the cuddling he'd suggested. Moments before he'd been cold and uncomfortable. But now he felt abundantly warm, almost too much so. He wouldn't be at all surprised if his damp clothing started to steam.

She was a very soft, very feminine weight nestled into his lap. And he really did enjoy her scent; something about it hit him on a gut level, very basic and primitive, forcing him to react in spite of himself. Overall, it was the kind of thing men fantasized about. Except for the kidnapping and the irritating storm.

"I was there to spy on someone."

He hadn't expected that, and the immediate conclusion he came to had a volatile effect on him. He stiffened, his voice sounding cold and hard even to his own ears. "A lover? A husband?"

She chuckled. "Nah, I have no interest in either of those, thank you very much." There was a heavy silence, then she added, "I suppose you could say I was actually spying for someone else."

"A friend?"

"Mmm. I didn't want anyone to recognize me."

"Well, you blundered into a mess and now I have to rescue you."

"Just like a fabled hero?" Her hair tickled his chin as she shook her head. "Not likely. I can take care of myself."

"I'm the first one to admit I'm not hero material. But I am bigger and stronger and I know the situation, whereas you're small and weak—"

She punched him in the stomach and he wheezed, then immediately flattened her against him so she couldn't retaliate further.

"—and you obviously don't know what you've gotten yourself into."

"Okay, so tell me. Who are these clowns who grabbed us and what are you going to do about it?"

He twisted to look down at her, and she lifted her face at the same time. Their noses bumped. Harry's thoughts scattered, and he struggled to bring them back to order. It wasn't easy.

"First I'm going to get you home and safe and out of my way. Then I'm going to get Floyd and Ralph, on my own ground, and pound some sense into them." He hesitated, pondering his own words and the probability of enacting them. "Maybe. I still have to weigh my personal vendetta against a promise I made to get them both legally stopped."

"A promise to who?"

"The friend who makes burnt sugar. He owns a shop in the area. Floyd and Ralph work for Carlyle as petty extortioners, and my friend refuses to pay. He's been threatened, and I don't take kindly to that sort of thing."

"What had you planned to do today?"

As she asked it, her gaze dropped to his mouth and one small hand opened on his chest. She looked vaguely confused, as if dealing with unfamiliar feelings. Harry understood completely, since he was in a similar predicament.

He forgot to answer her for the longest time. He could feel that small palm, warm and still, like a brand against his flesh. It aroused him, and surely that was insanity.

"Harry?"

He forcibly shored up his flagging wits. "Today I was just sizing things up." He touched her cheek where the bruise was visible, along with a little swelling. His tone lowered with regret. "Damn, I'm sorry you got hit."

"I've had worse."

Given her backbone and courage, he didn't doubt she'd led a hard life, but hearing of it made him want to hold her closer, to protect her. They stared at each other while Harry's fingers gently coasted over the bruise. If for no other reason than this, Floyd deserved to feel his fist, Harry decided.

"Answer me something, Charlie." His hand cupped her cheek and she didn't protest. He smoothed wet tendrils of hair away from her face, marveling at how soft her skin felt. Surely all women were as soft, but he couldn't seem to remember.

She didn't move away and he felt his heartbeat

thud, felt his muscles harden. "Did you mean what you said about not being interested? Not at all?"

Her gaze met his, so close. "Interested in what?"

"A lover."

"I don't know." She frowned, then looked at his mouth again. "I've never given it much thought."

He drew a slow breath, filling himself with her scent. "And now?"

She looked away, then back up again with a sort of daring grin. "I admit I'm thinking about it."

She was so bluntly honest, he smiled. Charlie might be demanding, but she would never be manipulative.

Her arms looped around his neck. "You know, Harry, this is turning into a romantic moment after all, isn't it?

Harry gently kissed the bruise on her cheek, his lips just grazing her skin, his nose nuzzling her temple. "Hmm. And I don't even have my flashlight out."

She chuckled. "I'm starting to like you, Harry."

It was the chuckle that did it, low and husky. He turned his face and she met him halfway and their mouths met, open and hot and devouring. *Oh damn*, Harry thought with some surprise. He hadn't expected this, hadn't thought she'd be this way, avaricious and hungry, clinging to him as if she'd never been kissed before or was starved for it. He was the starving one, and the hunger had come on him so suddenly.... It turned him on so much he groaned.

Sweeping one large hand down her back, he fondly cupped the adorable backside he'd admired earlier. Soft and sweet, the feel of her made him want more.

But before he could allow things to progress, he felt

he owed her a measure of honesty. "Charlie, honey, listen a minute. I have to tell you something."

Her eyes narrowed. "Getting discriminating on me again, Harry?"

He swallowed hard. Did she actually think he'd want to back out when he was shaking with lust? Not likely. "I'm not interested in a romantic relationship."

She blinked at him in surprise. "Okay." She tried to kiss him again, her hands clutching his shoulders.

He held her back with one hand, putting breathing space between them. "Charlie, I can't make you any promises."

She blinked twice, then frowned at him. "What are you talking about?"

She looked so confused he wanted to shake her. He realized his hand still held her bottom and he gave her a gentle squeeze, then shuddered with the effects of that caress. Damn, he wanted her. *Insane.*

"Marriage." He cleared his throat and managed to explain. "All those questions earlier. You were hinting about marriage and I want you to know, my plate is full right now. I have no intentions of getting even mildly involved with a woman."

One side of her mouth quivered, and she bit her lip. *Oh God, don't let her cry,* Harry thought, his body so tense he hurt, his mind feeling like mush.

She covered her mouth with her hand and a chuckle escaped. Harry frowned. In the next instant, her chuckles turned to uproarious laughter. "You," she said between hiccups, "thought I was sizing you up for marriage material?" She laughed some more, not dainty feminine laughter. No, this was boisterous, un-restrained hilarity. "Good grief, I hardly know you!"

Disgruntled with her misplaced mirth and his un-abated lust, Harry demanded, "Then why all the questions?"

"Actually, if you must know," she said, trying to get herself under control and failing miserably, "I had thought to *hire* you."

"Hire me for what, damn it?"

"To find out more information on my father." She wiped her eyes, perched primly on his lap with her midnight hair hung over one eye giving her a seduc-tive look. "That's what I was doing there today. Spy-ing on him. I haven't seen him in almost eighteen years."

Harry wanted explanations and he wanted them now. Who was her father? And why the long separa-tion?

His arms were still around her, one hand still splayed over perfect buttocks. When she smiled, her dark blue eyes seemed to smile, too.

He wished now that he'd kept his big mouth shut.

She traced his mouth with a delicate fingertip. "You really are a wonderful kisser, Harry."

Hope rose that he might be able to salvage this de-bacle, but then car lights hit the window of the gas sta-tion, and every thought other than protecting her slipped from his mind.

He shoved her off his lap and onto the dirty floor. "Stay there and don't make a sound." In the next sec-ond he was gone.

4

CHARLIE SAT ON the floor, her backside bruised, her lust squelched. Where had Harry gone? On hands and knees she crawled to the window to peek out. Just as her head lifted, Harry snatched it back down.

Hissing close to her ear, he asked, "Is there a particular reason you want to offer up your brains for target practice?"

"Where did you go?" Her words were muffled against his fly, and while there, she noticed he'd suffered quite a reaction to their kisses. Heaven help her, the man was hard.

"I was surveying our options, of course. Now be still."

She quit squirming and sighed. Having her cheek pressed to an erection, her nose smashed against a muscled thigh, with no hope of any loveplay, seemed like a terrible waste, especially since this was the first time in ages she'd been interested in such a thing. "Do you have any suggestions?"

"Yes, as a matter of fact, I do."

At that moment, Floyd called out. "You might as well come on out of there!"

Charlie whispered, "He certainly sounds furious."

"Yes, well, maybe he knows you planned to toss him off the truck."

"Ha! I think it's probably his aching jaw where you slugged him that has the bastard madder than hell."

He tsked. "Your language is a disgrace."

"You have my face buried in your lap, but you're worried about my language?"

Harry groaned, and his fingers contracted on the back of her head. "This is no time for your unregulated tongue, so keep quiet if you please."

"We know you're both in there!" Floyd growled. "There wasn't no place else for you to go. Now come on out and maybe we won't shoot you. We'll just take you to Carlyle."

Harry kept one large hand mashed against her head, forcing her to stay low, as he yelled out, "I have your gun, remember? Come anywhere near here and I'll be obliged to put a bullet in you! At the moment, the thought doesn't distress me at all."

Curses exploded from outside the garage.

"He really doesn't like you, Harry."

"The feeling is mutual, I assure you."

Unable to help herself, she nuzzled slightly into his lap. Harry jerked away. "Keep your head down, and no, don't say a thing. In case you've failed to notice, we're in something of a situation here. I need to keep my wits collected." When she dutifully remained silent, he nodded. "Good. Now, I'm going to draw them to the back of the garage. There's a door back there, and when they think we're escaping out the back, we'll make a run for the truck. Understand?"

He was all business, his eyes bright, his voice low, his body hard, poised for action. He impressed the hell out of Charlie, being so urbane one minute and so lethal the next.

"How can I help?"

"By not getting yourself killed. Now, do you understand everything I told you?"

"I'm not an idiot."

He sighed. "I suppose I'm to take that as a yes." He started to move away, then suddenly leaned forward and grabbed her by the neck. His mouth landed on hers, hot and hard, for the briefest second, and then he disappeared into the shadows. He managed to move without making a sound, causing her admiration to grow.

Charlie plopped down onto her backside and waited. She didn't like waiting. She felt ineffectual and cowardly and the feelings didn't rest well with her at all. She was used to taking action, to controlling things.

Floyd evidently didn't like waiting, either. "I'm losing patience!" he shouted. "I'll give you to the count of ten, then we're coming in and shooting any damn thing that moves. Carlyle would rather have you dead than loose."

Hurry up, Harry, she thought, listening as Floyd started a loud, monotonous recitation of his numbers.

Glass shattered at the back of the garage, followed by the sound of running footsteps. Cautiously, Charlie peeked over the edge of the window above her head. Floyd and Ralph stood frozen in the moonlight for a single heartbeat, then they cursed and ran hellbent for the back of the garage.

She waited until they were out of sight before she

slithered toward the door Harry had kicked in, proud of the fact that she, too, made no discernible noise. She'd barely edged outside before a rough, hot hand clamped over her mouth and a steely arm closed tight around her waist. She would have panicked if it hadn't been for Harry's height, assuring her he was the one who'd accosted her.

Without struggling, she got dragged to the truck and roughly thrust inside through the driver's door. Harry slid in beside her.

Seething, Charlie restraightened the huge coat she wore, holding the throat closed with a fist, and leaned close to whisper, "What? You thought I'd refuse your rescue and opt to stay with my buddy Floyd? Is that why you felt you had to manhandle—"

"No keys, damn it."

She squeaked. "What do you mean, no keys? How the heck are we going to—"

He thrust the gun into her hand. "Watch out for the two stooges while I hot-wire this barge."

Bemused, Charlie looked down at the gun in her hand, then to where Harry bent low beneath the dash, then dutifully out the window.

Hmm. There was something innately sexy about a man who could hot-wire.

It took him mere seconds. He'd just managed to fire the engine when Floyd and Ralph came stumbling back around the garage, their curses so hot Charlie's ears felt singed, and that was surely impressive given she'd been raised hearing curses all her life. The two men literally jumped up and down in rage as gravel and mud slung off the spinning tires, embellishing

Harry's daring getaway. Ralph fired, and Charlie thought she heard a bullet or two hit the side of the truck bed, but it didn't slow Harry. She waited, wondering if, because of the gunshot, he'd feel it necessary to put her head back in his lap.

She was slightly disappointed when he didn't.

Harry didn't say a word, concentrating instead on finding the main road and figuring out how to turn on the lights, the wiper blades, the heat. Charlie was just about to tuck the gun into her pocket when he retrieved it from her without a word.

She knew a struggle for the gun was useless, and she scowled. "Now what?"

Harry rubbed the back of his neck, glanced at her, his gaze moving over her from head to toe, then cursed slightly. "I think we'll abandon this truck outside town. No sense in taking a chance that Carlyle or one of his cronies will recognize it and want to pull us over. We'll grab a taxi to my apartment."

"Why your apartment?" Not that she'd complain. Her curiosity over Harry grew more rampant with every moment she spent in his company. From his place, she could call her sister, and then maybe they could finish what they'd started at the garage. She glanced down at Harry's lap, but the interior of the cab was too dark to tell if he still reacted to their little interlude. She liked it a lot that she'd turned him on. In all her life, she'd seldom had the opportunity, or the desire, to indulge in lust. But with Harry, well, she was more than a little intrigued.

"I think we need to talk, to figure out what we're going to do."

Charlie sighed, then carefully ventured a suggestion. "I don't think we should call the police."

Harry stilled for a moment, smoothly switched gears, then nodded. "Okay, I'll bite. Well, not really, not unless you wanted me to, and then it'd be more appropriate to say nibble—"

"Harry."

"Why don't you want to contact the police?"

"Because I can't see any way for you to explain this without telling them I was there, dressed as a guy, spying. And I'd just as soon no one knew about that."

"I can see where that would be a tale you'd hesitate to broadcast. But as it so happens I don't relish involving the police, either."

"And your reasons are?" When he only slanted her a look, she poked him in the side. "No way, Harry. I told, now it's your turn."

"You told very little, actually."

"I'll get into more detail once I'm warm and dry and have time to reason a few things out."

"I suppose that'll have to appease me."

"Give it up, Harry."

He didn't want to, she could tell that. He gave her a grudging look that almost made her smile. "I promised my friend I wouldn't involve any of the other people in the area. They're older proprietors, like Pops, and they aren't excessively fond of the police right now."

"You mean Pops—the guy who runs the store we were in before Floyd decided to play kidnapper?"

"That's right. They've contacted the police a few times in the past over other situations—loud music, loitering, things like that. They were pretty much told that since they're in a run-down, high-crime area, they have to expect a certain amount of that sort of thing. The police offered more surveillance, but the elders didn't think that was enough. They were determined to take matters into their own hands, which of course would be dangerous."

Even as she nodded, Charlie wondered if her father was one of the men being bothered. It seemed likely. She felt a moment's worry before she firmly squelched it. Her father deserved nothing but her enmity, and that's all he'd ever get. He'd never been there when she needed him most, but she'd found him now, and he could damn well pay. What she wanted from him—financial assistance to get her sister through college—had nothing to do with emotions or family relationships.

The rain started again, and they settled into a congenial quiet. Harry reached over and pulled her to his side. It wasn't quite as nice as his lap, but he was warm and firm and secure, and she took comfort from his nearness, though she'd never have admitted it.

As they neared the outskirts of town, Harry nudged her with his shoulder. "It's regretful things got interrupted back there."

"Yeah."

He cleared his throat. "If you're interested..."

"Yeah."

Laughing, Harry pulled the truck up to the curb and turned the engine off. He tilted Charlie's face up and kissed her softly. "There's nothing coy about you, is there?"

She raised a brow. "Should I pretend I'm not interested? That'd be dumb, Harry, since I don't get interested all that often."

Harry fought a smile, and lost. "So you're telling me you're not easy after all?"

Charlie snorted. "Most of the men that frequent my saloon could tell you I'm usually damn difficult."

"No! You? I'll never believe it."

Charlie smacked his shoulder. "Smart-ass."

Chuckling, Harry said, "Wait here. I'll call us a taxi."

He left the truck and trotted to a pay phone across the street. Charlie watched him go, admiring his long-legged stride, the way he held his head, the natural confidence and arrogance that appeared as obvious as his physical attributes. He was a strange man in many ways, his lofty wit and cultured diction in opposition to his easy acceptance at being kidnapped, shot at and holed up in a greasy garage. He'd stolen a truck as easily as if such a thing were a daily occurrence. Though it was apparent to Charlie he'd led an expensive, well-bred life, he hadn't so much as sniffed at her admission to owning a saloon, or the fact that for the most part, she was an obvious gutter rat, born and bred on the shadier side of life.

And he didn't hesitate to call her Charlie.

Most of the regulars at her saloon called her what she told them to, wary of getting on her bad side. They weren't, however, great examples of masculine humanity, so their concessions counted for very little. She had a feeling Harry, with all his grins and arrogance and stubbornness, was a true hero, even if he'd chosen to deny it.

He watched her from the phone booth while he placed the call, alert to any possible danger. With a smile, Charlie turned away to view their surroundings. They were near a park, but not one she recognized. Of course, she had little time or interest for dawdling in parks, so that wasn't a surprise.

Seconds later, Harry returned. His wet dress shirt clung to his upper torso, showing a large, smoothly muscled chest and shoulders, and even through his undershirt, she could see a sprinkling of chest hair. The shirt opened at the collar and his strong throat was wet, a couple of droplets of rain rolling down into the opening. Charlie swallowed.

His damp hair stuck to his nape and one brown lock hung over his brow. His light brown eyes, framed by spiked eyelashes, darkened as he watched her inspect his features. Harry leaned back on the seat and the corners of his mouth tipped in a slight smile. "Have I sprouted horns?"

Charlie shook her head. "You're a real looker."

One brow lifted as his smile turned into a grin. "Thank you."

"I bet you hear that a lot."

"Seldom enough to keep me humble."

She choked on a laugh. "There's not a humble bone in your big body, Harry, and I bet women fawn over you all the time."

He didn't deny it. He did tilt his head to look at her, then slowly reached out to touch the top button of his coat, where it rested low on her chest. "I don't suppose you'd want to pass the time by appeasing my curiosity over these mysterious breasts of yours, would you?"

Charlie gaped. She should have been used to his boldness by now, especially since his brain did seem to stay focused on her upper assets—or lack thereof. "You expect me to just flash the coat open for your entertainment?"

He shrugged, shifted to his side to face her. His finger trailed over the deep V at the neck of the coat, tickling her skin, raising her body temperature by several degrees. "I'll admit I'm vastly interested, and while you're indulging in more temperate humors, I thought this might be the ideal time. Besides, what else have you got to do right now other than model for my delectation?"

He certainly had a way with words. And his gentle touch and tone, compared to the coarseness she was accustomed to, was a major turn on. But she shook her head. "I'm not putting on a show for you, Harry, so forget it."

Harry fought his grin. "Ah, well, you do like to vex a man, don't you?"

Before she could answer, headlights flashed against the windshield of the truck. For a second there, Charlie panicked, thinking somehow Floyd and Ralph had found them. But then Harry leaned forward, gave her a swift kiss, and said, "Our ride is here. Faster than I'd anticipated, but evidently the cabbie was in the area. Come on. Other than seeing your elusive bosom, dry clothing is the most appealing thing on my mind."

The cabbie, a seasoned veteran, made no comment

on her lack of shoes or bedraggled appearance, much to Charlie's relief. Harry somehow managed to be imperious, despite their circumstances, and the driver gave him due deference.

Harry held her hand all the way to his apartment, which wasn't all that far, taking a mere fifteen minutes. But it was long enough to make her edgy, to make her ponder several different things, mostly how enticing the thought of having an affair with him seemed.

He paid the cabbie, refusing to let her dig money from her own pocket to pay half. In fact, he seemed insulted by the very idea. Charlie shrugged. She needed her money, and if he wanted to play the gallant, that was fine by her.

Harry led her to the first floor of an exclusive complex, and Charlie wasn't at all surprised to see, once he'd gotten the door unlocked, that his apartment wasn't an apartment at all, but rather an expensively decorated, immaculate and beautiful town house. She couldn't help herself, she felt intimidated.

Then the barking began, startling her half out of her skin.

Harry relocked the door and switched on more lights. A miniature collie and a small, stocky, mixed-breed mutt darted out around a large, beige leather sofa. The collie's entire body quivered with happiness at the sight of Harry and he laughed as the dog jumped up and down in near berserk joy. The mutt, a little more subdued, ran circles around Harry and howled. Harry immediately knelt to rub the dog's scruff. He glanced up at Charlie. "Meet Grace and

Sooner. Grace has been with me a long time, but Sooner has only been in the family a couple of years."

She stared at the dogs, who stared back, one sitting on each side of Harry, heads tilted, expressions alert, like sentinels guarding the king from a scourge. She grinned, and the dogs seemed to grin back.

"I can understand the name Grace, since she looks so refined. But Sooner?"

Harry shrugged. "He'd 'sooner' be one breed as another."

"Ah."

Harry patted the dogs. "She's entirely acceptable, guys, so you may as well present her with the royal treatment."

Once he said it, both dogs trotted over to sniff her, lick her hand, bark a few times in a doggy greeting. Then they each gave Harry a quizzical look, as if her presence made no sense at all, and retreated. Grace leaped up to lie on the sofa, resting her head on a black and beige motif throw folded over one end. Sooner went over to flop onto the floor in front of a white stone electric fireplace. He gave a loud groan and closed his eyes.

The town house was very sleek, and as Charlie looked around, she saw marble-topped oak end tables, bare wood floors with thick area rugs, and windows with streamlined blinds rather than curtains. All in all, she thought the room was gorgeous and suited Harry to a T.

She was afraid to move. Her bare feet were muddy, grime from the garage between her white toes. Water still dripped from her hair, her nose, Harry's coat. She felt like a flea-ridden squirrel turned loose in a palace.

No wonder the dogs thought her curious.

"Make yourself at home. I'll locate us some dry clothes. Would you like something to drink?"

All the social niceties. Charlie shook her head, fighting the urge to fidget. "I'd really like to call and check in with my sister, if you don't mind."

He went to a desk situated in front of a long window that looked out over the backyard. It was partially separated from the living room by a wide arched doorway. Charlie could see oak file cabinets and office equipment. She heard Harry curse.

"What's wrong?"

"The electricity evidently went out with the storm. My answering machine is dead, meaning I've missed any calls that may have come in."

"Were you expecting an important call?"

"Several, actually." He walked back to her. "You'll have to use the phone in my bedroom. The portable is out."

His bedroom?

Harry crossed his arms over his wet chest and frowned at her. "Surely that look doesn't mean you're afraid of me? Not the woman who challenged Floyd and Ralph, the woman who did her best to bait two miscreants. I assure you, you're safe enough with me."

"Me, fear you? Ha!" She was more afraid of herself at the moment. She felt like tossing his gorgeous self to the floor and having her way with him. But she would never do such a thing in front of the innocent dogs.

"It's just that my feet are dirty. The dogs are cleaner than I am. I don't want to track mud all over the place."

Harry looked down, took in her bare feet and growled. "I forgot you'd removed those hideous boots. You could have cut yourself on something when we ran for the truck. I can't believe I didn't notice sooner. Well, actually I can, given my attention was somewhat fractured by other things, but not so much so, I shouldn't have noticed naked feet. I am a P.I. after all, usually very alert to small details."

"Uh, Harry?"

He still stared at her feet. "Hmm?"

"The phone?"

"Oh, yes, of course. Okay, no help for it. I suppose I'll have to play the martyr."

"No! Don't you dare... Harry, put me down."

"You're really very slight, now that we've rid you of your ridiculous waterlogged costume." As he made his way up a flight of carpeted stairs, he looked down at her, their noses almost touching, and the smile he gave her made her catch her breath. His gaze dipped lower, and Charlie glanced down to see the coat had slipped some and she had a modest amount—all she possessed really—of cleavage showing. She tried to make a grab for the coat, but then Harry lowered her, and she realized she was in a taupe and black tiled bathroom, more specifically, he stood her in the black tub.

"Don't move. I'll play lady's maid and get you a towel and dry clothes and you can clean up just a bit before we progress any further."

Progress to what, she wondered? Another part of his home, or another level of intimacy? She knew where her vote would be, but she didn't say so. She did need to clean up, and dry clothes sounded heavenly.

Harry reappeared with two plush white towels, a long polo shirt, and silky boxer shorts. He grinned as he laid the items on the marble vanity. "The thing is, you're something of a squirt, so nothing I have would be small enough to fit you. However, I wear a "tall" so my shirt should make do for a dress, only I couldn't bear the thought of you being naked beneath it, not if you expect me to exhibit my more civilized tendencies, so I determined the boxers would serve as well as anything." He lifted his hands. "I'm fresh out of ladies' panties."

She drew a blank, except to ask, "You wear silk boxers?"

"Actually no. They were a gift from a friend."

"Ah."

He headed for the door. "Go ahead and wash up. You can hang the coat on the back of the door and I'll take care of it later. There's a hamper under the cabinet where you can stick your muddy jeans. I'll be in the kitchen making coffee after I've changed."

The second he was out the door, Charlie rushed through her bath. She stripped off the coat, praying it wasn't ruined, and then spent several minutes working her wet, worn jeans down her legs. She didn't know what to do with her panties—no way would she put them in his hamper for him to find later. After giving it some thought, she washed them out and hung them on the side of the tub.

She disdained a full shower for simply cleaning herself off. Calling her sister was a priority.

Once she'd pulled on the dry clothes Harry'd brought her, she found his comb and worked the tangles out of her short hair. The polo shirt hung almost to her knees, looking, as he'd predicted, like a dress. It adequately covered her, but the silky boxers tickled. Rather than toss her dirty jeans in the hamper as he'd suggested, she folded them, put her panties in the pocket along with her money, and left the bathroom.

Harry sat on a corner of a colossal bed, head bent forward while he towel-dried his hair. He had on clean khaki slacks, and nothing else. His back was broad, muscled, lightly tanned. His feet were long, narrow, braced apart on the thick carpeting. Charlie stood there gawking, appreciating what a spectacular sight he made.

Oh yes, she definitely wanted to explore these unique feelings he inspired. She'd been around men all her life, but she'd never, not once, felt this much interest in one.

Her sigh caught his attention. He lifted his head, surveyed her tip to toes, then slowly stood. "You are an adorable sight, Charlie..." He paused, looking much struck. "I just realized I don't know your last name."

"Jones," she squeaked, breathless over the way he watched her. She cleared her throat. "Charlie Jones."

He held out his hand in the formal, time-honored tradition. "Harry Lonnigan." Smiling, she stepped forward, shifted her wet jeans to one arm, and took his hand. With a mere glimpse of evil intent, Harry tugged her forward. He took her small bundle from her and dropped it to the floor. His hands lifted to cradle her face, she caught her breath, and then he kissed her.

HARRY COULDN'T believe the way she made him feel. It was a simple kiss, damm it, and heaven knew he'd kissed plenty of women in his time. And among those women, Charlie was likely the least proficient at it. So her lips were soft? So she smelled incredibly sweet?

She looked like a rumpled child in his shirt, the shoulders bagging almost to her elbows, the hem skimming her knees—very sexy knees actually, followed by shapely calves. He shook his head. She'd combed her hair straight back, evidently not the least interested in impressing him with her feminine attributes. She'd made no effort at all to make herself more appealing. Yet he already had an erection and he practically shook with lust. All because of a simple kiss.

It was so unexpected, he almost grinned.

That happened a lot with her; hell, he'd grinned more since first spotting her in that small grocery, all decked out like an adolescent thug, than he had in the past six months.

Beneath his palms, her skin warmed and she felt so incredibly silky, so vibrant, he wanted to devour her. *He never devoured women!* He was suave and controlled and applauded for his technique.

She had him so turned on, he couldn't even remember his touted technique.

His thumbs stroked over her temple, her jaw. He kept the kiss easy, letting her lead, though he wanted badly to taste her, to slip his tongue into her mouth, to feel her tongue on his.

With a groan, he pulled back the tiniest bit and looked at her. Eyes almost closed, she swayed toward him, her pale, flushed skin in striking contrast to her glossy black hair and dark blue eyes. Her lips were slightly parted, and unable to help himself, he kissed her again, this time giving in to the urge to explore. He licked over her lips, and when she gasped, he slipped inside, coasting over her teeth, mating with her soft tongue.

He pulsed with need, he was so aroused.

Charlie's hands opened on his naked shoulders. She moved against him, and he could feel her stiff little nipples, could feel the plumpness of her breasts, small, but very feminine and sweet. He started to lift a hand, to cup her, tease her and himself, and his honor came knocking, just barely nudging aside the need.

Unspoken invective filled his brain. He wanted so badly to feel her breasts, but...

Once he got started, he knew good and well it would be hours before he got his fill. He should be getting in touch with Dalton. He had no doubts the man would be worried, wondering what had transpired, whether or not Harry had been able to make any headway. He owed Dalton that much.

"Charlie."

"Hmm..." She nuzzled his throat, took a small nip of his chin.

"Sweetheart, we need to talk."

She blinked up at him, her look dreamy. "You called me sweetheart."

Sighing, he said again, "We need to talk. Now."

She stiffened, her gaze searching his. "Oh good grief. Please, don't give me the old 'you're not that kind of guy' routine."

He took two steps back, and commended himself for accomplishing that much when he wanted so badly to feel her flush against him.

"I'm absolutely that kind of guy," he assured her, staring down into her sweet face. "I'm the kind of guy who is nearly desperate to strip you to your very sexy naked hide. I'm the kind of guy that once I got started, especially on the unveiling on these stupendous breasts of yours, I wouldn't want to stop until we were both insentient and without wit. I wouldn't stop until you begged me to. Unfortunately, what happened to-night probably has several people worrying about us."

The changing expressions on her face were almost comical. She went from openmouthed surprise, to blushing, to wide-eyed with realization. "My sister!"

"Yes. And I have a friend to contact. They deserve to know that we're still alive and kicking."

She rudely shoved him aside to snatch up the phone, and Harry admired the smooth rounded lines of her delectable backside. Nobility was surely a curse.

"I can't believe I forgot about my sister." She sent him a grave look of accusation and dialed the phone, muttering how it was his fault for distracting her, leaving off his shirt, showing his bare feet.

His bare feet? Harry shook his head. There was no accounting for her strange twists of reason. "I'll finish dressing while you make your call."

She'd barely finished dialing when Harry heard a shouted, frantic "hello" through the earpiece. Her sister had evidently been waiting for the call.

"Jill...I know, and I'm so sorry. I'm fine, really— *Jill, I'm fine,* I promise. Well, it's a long story. I met a guy... No, Jill, it's not *that* long." Charlie glared at him, and Harry took the hint. He grabbed the rest of his clothes and left the room with a salute.

As he bounded down the stairs, he could hear the animated conversation, along with the occasional hushed, whispering tones, which he assumed meant the two women were discussing him. He entered the kitchen and because he was distracted, he almost tripped over his cat, Ted, now twisting around his bare ankles. It didn't matter where Ted might be, if Harry entered the kitchen, Ted showed up.

He smiled down at the cat as he added some fresh food to his dish—always the first order of business. "I wonder how much Charlie will actually tell of our adventure."

The dogs heard him talking and sauntered in. Harry reached for the back door which led to a tiny yard with a privacy fence. "Hey, why don't you guys go out and run around a little, maybe give me some privacy?"

Doggy tails wagged, but actual bodies didn't move.

The cat looked thoroughly indignant at such a suggestion and continued to eat.

"So it rained a little. Don't you have to go?"

Sooner woofed an agreement and ran out. Grace took a little more coaxing, until she heard Sooner bark again and trotted out to investigate. Ted, with a look of disdain, licked his whiskers clean and leaped up to sit in one of the kitchen chairs.

Harry had the coffee ready, two cups poured, when Charlie came striding in. Harry handed her a cup and motioned for her to sit at the round table. Unfortunately, she tried to sit in Ted's chair.

Ted could be very theatrical when it suited him. He made a horrid hissing sound, arched his back, fuzzed out his tail and made a general threatening display until Charlie had backed up a good five feet.

"What the hell's wrong with your cat?"

Harry smiled fondly at his pet. "That's Ted. He doesn't like females."

"Ted? How'd you come up with that name?"

Shrugging, he said, "He's just Ted. Here, use this chair."

Cautiously, keeping her gaze on the cat, Charlie circled to the chair Harry held out. "Is he always so mean?"

"With women, yes. He behaves well enough for me. Or maybe I behave well enough to suit him. Whatever, the arrangement works." Harry smiled at her.

"The dogs don't bother him?"

"Actually, they all get along fairly well. On his first day here, about a year or so ago, Ted explained things. We haven't had a real ruckus since."

"You've only had him a year? He looks older."

"He is. I found him in an alley while I was on a job.

He saved me by making a grand distraction when he objected to our invasion of his private space."

"He threw a hissy like he just did to me?"

"Exactly, which effectively distracted the fellow who'd been holding a gun on me. I was able to...get the upper hand. So I brought Ted home. The vet treated him, despite Ted's vicious complaints, and as long as I keep him well fed and his litter box clean, he doesn't destroy my home."

"A fair enough trade-off, I suppose." She still eyed the cat warily, but Harry was pleased to see there was no dislike in her eyes. She understood, and he liked that.

"Cream or sugar?"

She snorted at such a suggestion, then took a healthy sip of her black coffee.

Harry scrutinized her as he liberally sweetened his own. "So you drink yours like a trucker, hmm? Now why doesn't that surprise me?"

After another sip, she asked, "For the same reason that seeing you turn yours into syrup doesn't surprise me?"

"Your insults are getting sloppier. You must be tired." He glanced at the clock, saw it was after midnight, and wondered if he should call Dalton after all. He hated to wake the older man if he'd already gone to bed. And Dalton did know Harry could take care of himself, so perhaps he hadn't been worried at all. "Is your sister appeased by whatever story you told her?"

She frowned at that. "I told her the truth, and yeah, she's appeased, but far from happy. She told me she's going to wait up for me."

Charlie offered that last small tidbit with a wince, which told Harry the night was going to get a whole lot shorter. "I assume this means you want to head home soon?"

"I'm afraid so. Jill is only eighteen, and she worries more than she should."

That brought out a snort, which appalled him. Good God, he was beginning to pick up her less discriminating habits. Harry cleared his throat. "More than she should? With a sister who muddles into extortion and gets herself kidnapped, I'd say she's justified."

Charlie shrugged. "She wants me to give it up, my spying that is, but I'm determined."

"Charlie—"

"No, before you start any lectures, I have a few questions for you."

"Please, don't keep me in suspense."

"I know you said you wouldn't want to see me again—"

Before he could correct her, because at this point he had every intention of seeing her, all of her, as many times as was necessary to get the fever out of his system, she held up a hand and continued.

"Don't worry. I'm not going to get clingy. A little hanky-panky would have been...nice. But the night has gotten way too complicated, and I can see why you wouldn't want to get involved with me beyond the night. I mean, we're hardly two peas from the same pod." She tried a smile that looked more like a grimace. "But... Well, I was hoping we could work out a different arrangement."

Harry leaned back in his seat, positively prostrated.

"You think a rendezvous with me would be merely *nice?*"

She looked startled by his tone. "*Very* nice," she clarified, as if that made it better.

He felt smote to his masculine core. Here he'd been dredging up pagan images too erotic to bear, and she'd relegated the possibilities to merely *nice.* "I'll have you know—"

"I'd like to hire you, Harry."

That effectively put the brakes on his righteous diatribe. Hire him? Did she consider him a gigolo? Did she dare think she could afford him if he *was* for sale? The nerve.

But in a lusty sort of way the idea genuinely appealed to him. His body tensed until his muscles cramped. He was so hard, he could be considered a weapon.

Carefully, in case he misunderstood, he asked, "Hire me for what?"

"Detecting, of course. What else would I mean?"

Disappointment flowed through him. Nevertheless, he contrived to look merely curious. "Of course. And what would you need a P.I. for?"

"I told you." she said with exaggerated patience. "To find out information on my father. He abandoned my sister and me ages ago, and that's fine by me because from what I know of it, we were better off without him. Except now I think it's time he accepted a few responsibilities. I figure since your friend has hired you to look into the extortion, and my father is one of the proprietors in that area, it shouldn't really be too much trouble for you to find out a few things for me."

A sick feeling of dread started to choke him. He remembered their most recent introduction, when she'd given him her last name. His belly churned, and he forced the question out. "Your father is?"

"Dalton Jones."

5

HARRY STARTED TO choke, picked up his coffee to take a large gulp, then choked some more. Coffee spewed out his nose and Charlie jumped up to pound on his back with surprising force. The cat hissed and loped out of the room. Harry fumbled for a napkin, and while Charlie tried to drive his ribs through his chest, he cleaned his face.

"You okay?"

Wheezing, he said, "If you'd quit bludgeoning me, it's possible I'll survive."

She quit. In fact, her small hand opened, and rather than pounding, she smoothed her palm over his back. Harry stiffened. "What are you doing?" he asked carefully.

"You feel nice. Hard. And real warm."

He started to choke again, and Charlie reseated herself. "That was the strangest damn thing, Harry. I've never seen coffee shoot out someone's nose before. And it was still steaming." She looked vaguely impressed when she added, "That had to hurt."

"You frightened Ted, attacking me that way—"

"Yeah, right." She gave a hearty snort. "Nothing would scare that beast."

"—and you don't sound the least bit sympathetic, so just be quiet." His brain throbbed not only from her interested, caressing touch, but with ramifications of her admission. Dalton Jones, his best friend, the man who'd always been there for him, emotionally supported him, got him through his divorce-from-hell, was Charlie's father? And she didn't appear to have any fond feelings for the man. No, she literally sneered when she said his name, leading Harry to believe her feelings bordered more on contempt than anything else. Harry dropped his head to a fist and sighed.

"Sheesh. What's got you so all-fired dejected, Harry?" She lounged back in the chair, at her leisure. "If you don't want the job, just say so. It's not like I was trying to coerce you or anything. I just thought since you'll be checking things out there anyway, it'd be no big deal to let me know if you heard anything."

Feeling himself duly cornered, Harry sighed again. "Let me get this straight. You want to get reacquainted with your father?" It was a shock, but Dalton would certainly be thrilled. Harry knew he'd spent a good portion of his life chasing after his ex-wife, doing his best to locate his children, to reclaim them, but the woman had always eluded him for reasons of her own.

Charlie bristled like an offended porcupine. "Hell no! I personally don't want anything to do with him. And if I had any other choices, he could rot for all I cared. But...well, my mother passed away not too long ago and between her never-ending medical bills and the funeral, I'm flat broke. I need some cash to get my sister through college. The bar is mortgaged through the roof, and I can't handle another personal loan."

Harry started to tell her that Dalton would gladly help her in any way he could. But he held back. It wasn't his place to make promises for Dalton, so he decided to talk to him first. Besides, Charlie's attitude was less than promising, and explaining away the past was a chore Dalton could better handle.

Still, Harry felt he had to soften her just a bit, to perhaps suggest she modify her assumptions until the facts could be presented. "I'm sorry to hear about your financial difficulties, but—"

Her fist smacked the tabletop, causing him to jump. "Why should my sister have to settle for less than the college of her choice, just because my father was too low, too deceitful to own up to his responsibilities? Why should he get off leaving the entire burden to me...I mean, my mother?"

Harry heard the slip, of course, but he let it pass. All he knew about Charlie's mother was what Dalton had shared, and he imagined from what he'd heard, Charlie's life hadn't been an easy one. That had been one of the biggest motivators for Dalton, the main reason why he'd refused to give up the search. He'd worried endlessly for the well-being of his daughters.

The dogs chose that propitious moment to want in, giving Harry a few minutes to think. He automatically went into his laundry room first to get an old towel, then opened the back door and knelt down. The dogs, well used to the routine, waited while Harry cleaned their muddy paws.

Charlie gawked at him. "Do you do that every time they go out?"

"When necessary, yes. I have fastidious dogs."

"Gee, I wonder where they get it from?"

There was just enough sarcasm in her tone to tell Harry she was nettled. Very slowly, he looked up at her. "You're not, perchance, making fun of my animals, are you?"

Her brows lifted.

"Because while I'll accept aspersions thrown at me, I don't take kindly to insults of my pets."

She rolled her eyes. "You're defending an old collie, a mutt and an alley cat?"

His eyes narrowed and she muttered, "All right. Sorry."

She didn't look overly sincere. In fact, she still looked angry. Well, there was nothing he could do about it, not yet at least.

Harry reseated himself. Sooner laid on the floor, resting his head on Harry's feet. Grace went to her dish to eat. "Perhaps your father has a legitimate excuse—"

"Ha! If he does, then he can damn well keep it to himself, because I'm not interested in hearing it. Years ago I might have..." Her voice trailed off and she looked away. Sooner stared at her, picked up on her distress, and abandoned his master to go lick her hand. Charlie smiled and scratched his head.

After an audible swallow, she continued. "All I want to know is if he's got any money, if I can count on him to do the right thing. He owes it to my sister to help her, to give her the opportunity to do her best in this world."

Harry saw her stubborn pride, her visible struggle to keep herself together. Something inside him softened, and that tender feeling made him uneasy. "What about you? Doesn't he owe you, too, Charlie?"

She stared him straight in the eye and said, "If it was just me, I'd gladly survive in the gutter with the moldy rats before giving him the time of day."

Well. Harry leaned back in his seat, nonplussed. She certainly had a visual way of getting her point across. "Things aren't always as they seem, you know."

She stood, and both Grace and Sooner flanked her. "If you don't want to help out, that's fine. But spare me the lectures on goodwill. My charitable attitude died a long time ago."

She turned away and the dogs followed, forming a small parade. Harry felt abandoned and left his seat to hurry after them. Since his legs were so long, he only had to hurry for two steps. "Where are you going?"

"To call a cab. It's time for me to head home."

"Charlie." He caught her arm and turned her back around to face him. But she looked up at him, and her face was so innocent, despite her bravado, her eyes dark and searching, he felt that damn tender feeling swell up again. It seemed to explode inside him, filling him up, choking him when he hadn't even touched his cursed coffee.

He released her and backed up. The dogs frowned at him, but with the facts of her parentage dropped at his feet, all carnal tendencies would have to be forgotten. He couldn't see her as a sexual being, as a woman he wanted so badly his muscles ached. No, she was the daughter of his friend, a man who'd always been like a father figure to Harry. Touching her would mean betraying Dalton, and he couldn't do that.

Charlie was definitely off-limits.

That little truism annoyed his libido and gnawed at his control, but he stiffened his resolve.

He shook his head, verifying to himself, if not to her, that he couldn't, *wouldn't*, be tempted. Not now. "I'll drive you home. You can't very well get into a cab alone this time of night, especially not dressed like that."

She summoned a look of such scorn, he felt his ears burn. "I know how to take care of myself, Harry. I've been doing it most of my life. You can rest easy. Your duty is over."

He looked down his nose at her, being deliberately intimidating, which sent the dogs slinking off, though the effect on her seemed minimal. "Your shoulders are too narrow to support such an enormous chip, Charlie. No, don't flog me with your insults. I *am* taking you home and that's all there is to it. Since I'm of a greater size, and you're rather piddling in comparison, it stands to reason I'm more capable of carrying through with any threats, veiled or otherwise. It'll be better for both of us if whatever you're thinking remains unsaid."

She rolled her eyes. "Half the time, Harry, I have no idea what the hell you're saying."

"And...," he added, knowing he was jumping into a muddy creek when he had no idea how deep it might be, "I will check into things for you."

There, he'd committed himself. But even as he'd reluctantly uttered the ill-fated words, Harry wondered
what else he could possibly have done. He couldn't
just let her leave; Dalton would never forgive him.
He'd looked for his children, spent a small fortune on
the chore, for a great many years. Now here was his
daughter, despising Dalton without knowing him, re-
senting him on hearsay, condemning him without
knowing all the details, and Harry had the chance to
find out where she lived, to assure Dalton that his
daughters were alive and thriving.

He thought of everything at stake, and added softly,
"Please, Charlie."

It was the "please" that did it, causing the rigidity in
her shoulders to relax, her attitude to soften enough
that she could agree. "Oh, all right," she muttered,
without an ounce of feigned graciousness. "I suppose
it doesn't make sense to give up what I want just because I'm pissed off."

She was certainly direct. "Ah...exactly." He retrieved
her jeans and found her another jacket to keep her
warm on the ride to her place. They both said goodbye
to the dogs, who wanted badly to go along but Harry
explained to them there wasn't room. "Just guard the
place until I come home."

The dogs went back to sleeping in their self-
appointed spots.

Ted was nowhere to be found.

"He sulks when it's dark," Harry explained, "because more than anything, he likes lazing around in
the sunshine. When there is none, Ted hides. Which is

good, because when he doesn't hide, he makes his discontent known to everyone."

Charlie gave him a soft, feminine look that took him completely off-guard. "You're very good to them, Harry."

He didn't like that look, didn't want her thinking soft, feminine things about him, not when he couldn't do anything about it. So he hustled her out to the parking garage where he kept his car before temptation could get the better of him, or before she could start disagreeing with him again. She truly was a most contrary woman.

He worried about her being barefoot, but he certainly had no shoes that would stay on her small feet, and she'd disdained the socks he offered her. Luckily, the complex was kept tidy, with nothing strewn about the grounds to injure her tender skin. No broken glass or debris.

She had very cute feet.

"You know, Harry, I figured you'd left your car at the grocery today."

Distracted from her pink toes—hardly a source of sexual stimulation, even if his body tended to disagree—he looked up at her and made a face. "My car wouldn't have survived three minutes parked at that curb. I took a taxi. What about you?"

"The bus. Cabs are a little out of my price range."

As he stopped next to his car, a shiny black Jaguar convertible, she dug in her bare heels, stiffened up again, and whistled low. "*These* are your wheels?"

"Yes." He noticed her horrified expression and patiently asked, "Now what's the problem?"

She turned to him, beautiful blue eyes wide, jaw dropped. "I can't afford you! First that luxury town house, and now this. You must make a killing as a P.I. to afford this car. I mean, these suckers go for over fifty grand a pop!"

Her phraseology alternately amused and irritated him, but her meaning was always quite clear. After another heartfelt sigh, Harry opened the door and practically thrust her inside. "Put on your seat belt." He closed the door, circled the car and slid behind the wheel.

Her frown was ferocious. "I mean it, Harry. We need to reevaluate here. I thought it'd cost a few hundred bucks at the most to get your help. I had no idea—"

The car started with a throaty purr. "I'm not charging you, Charlie."

He was in the middle of backing up when she opened her car door and literally leaped out. He slammed on the brakes. "What in the name of—"

She leaned in and growled across the seat, "I don't take charity, Harry Lonnigan!" He opened his mouth, and she said, "And before you bother sighing again, let me tell you, this is *not* negotiable!"

Since Harry had lost all semblance of patience, he barked, "Fine. Have it your way. But a few hundred will more than cover it, so get your sweet little posterior back in the damn car!" He ended on a shout, and shouting was something Harry had seldom done since his divorce. He liked it that way, liked his life calm and orderly, dished up to his specific design, without interruptions and disturbances and ill-mannered females throwing things into a whirlwind and stirring up unaccountable lust.

He sucked in a deep breath, sought for lost control, and continued in a forced icy-polite tone, "I have inherited money from my father, and that's how I bought the car. Now, will you please quit making a spectacle of yourself and let me drive you home?"

She gingerly reseated herself, as if the leather seat could bite her. She also looked around the garage, then snorted at him. "I can hardly be a spectacle when there's no one here to see."

"I'm here, and your show is beyond distressing. A little decorum wouldn't kill you, you know."

She relatched her seat belt, then waited until they'd entered the nearly abandoned roadway before saying, "So you come from a rich family, huh? I could have guessed that."

Harry looked at her with acute dislike. His father had been rich, and he'd also been unfeeling. He'd given Harry very little during his life, certainly no real emotion or pride or concern. Taking his wealth after his death had been beyond difficult. At first, all Harry'd wanted to do was give it away. But Dalton convinced Harry to accept his father's legacy, to acknowledge and use the one thing his father had been capable of sharing.

He didn't discuss his father with anyone but Dalton, certainly not with a woman he'd only known a day, a woman who seemed to take pleasure in pricking him, both his mind and his body. "You're an irritant, Charlie. Now would you like to give me directions or should I try guessing?"

"Go to the corner of Fifth and Elm. You can see my bar from there. It's called the Lucky Goose. There's a big sign hanging out front, painted in lime green."

That description alone was enough to make his stomach queasy. "You must be joking."

"Nope." She sent him an impish smile and added, "Lime is the dominant shade in our decorating scheme. Not too long ago, I had to replace several things, and I found a lot of stuff at an auction, real cheap."

"Whenever something is 'real cheap,' there's usually a viable reason why."

She laughed. "You're right about that. The lime is almost enough to make you toss your breakfast, especially with so much of it. But the men who frequent my bar aren't out for the fashionable ambiance. They're there to drown their supposed woes, and as long as they have a stool to sit on and a glass in front of them, they can forgive anything else. And to be real honest with you, the color's kind of grown on me. I figure if I ever get far enough ahead, I'll add some black accent pieces. That'd look good, don't you think? Sort of classy? Black and lime?"

Harry shuddered with the image. *I'll tell Dalton how witty Charlie is, how spunky, how energetic. I'll simply leave out her appalling lack of taste.* When she continued to stare at him, waiting for his response, Harry forced a smile. "Yes, charming."

She beamed at him.

"Tell me about your sister."

"What about her?"

"I don't know. Anything, everything. Does she help you in the bar, things like that."

Charlie turned to look out the window. "Jillian just turned eighteen. She's beautiful, so intelligent she scares me sometimes, sweet, giving. She's also naive and a worrier." Charlie turned back to face him, her expression earnest. "And no, I would never let her work in the bar. That's why I need the money so she can go to college. She's gotten some partial academic scholarships, but not enough to foot the whole bill. If I left it up to her, she'd put off going for a year and save the difference herself, and even then, she'd have to settle for a less expensive college, and she'd lose the partial scholarships. I don't want her to have to do that. She's worked too hard all these years, keeping her grade average up, excelling in all her classes. She deserves the best, and one way or another, she's going to have it."

It was that *one way or another* that had Harry worried.

They rode the rest of the way in companionable silence. The late moon was partially hidden by clouds, not a star in sight. The near empty roads were still wet and the tires made a slick hissing sound that could lull a turbulent mind.

And then that damn glaring green sign jumped out at him. Charlie hadn't told him it was framed with a neon green gaslight. The color was so bold, it seemed to throb in nauseating waves through the darkness. Cautiously, surveying the area, Harry pulled up to the curb. He swallowed hard, not wanting to ask but knowing he had to. "So, this is the bar. But where do you live?"

"Upstairs." She unhooked her seat belt. "When I bought the place, the second floor was empty, so I converted it into an apartment. My mother was already sick then, so I needed to work close to her and Jillian. The setup is great, though I wasn't crazy about having Jillian at a bar. But the stairs leading up are just inside the door, so Jillian doesn't have to come all the way into the bar unless she wants to. There's a door at both the bottom and top of the stairs, and they're kept locked. Only Jillian and I have keys. Anybody I see messing around with the door gets tossed out and isn't welcomed back. Since the Lucky Goose is so popular, nobody wants to test me on it."

That strange tenderness swelled in his chest again, making him warm and fidgety. "You're a real tough guy, aren't you, Charlie?"

He said it softly, working the words out around the lump in his throat, but she took him literally. She shoved the door open and climbed out. "I have to be."

She looked surprised when he turned off the engine, stepped out, and activated his car alarm.

"What do you think you're doing?"

Harry grinned. "A gentleman always sees a lady to her door."

She looked nearly frantic with consternation. "I'll agree you're a gentleman, Harry, but I'm hardly a *lady*. You can save your gallantry for someone who'll appreciate it. I don't need to be seen anywhere."

Her denials made that strange tenderness more acute, almost like a pain. She was so used to taking care of herself, with no help at all. She was a small woman, but she gave the impression of being an amazon with her stubborn, forceful attitude. It hurt to think of all she'd been through before perfecting that attitude.

Shaking off the feeling, Harry took her arm and began ushering her reluctantly forward. "You look more than feminine to me." Especially since he knew she wore his silk boxers beneath the long shirt. His palms itched with the need to smooth that slippery material over her sweetly rounded bottom. *No, no, no. Dalton's daughter, Dalton's daughter...* He mentally repeated that litany until his heart calmed.

As they stepped inside the heavy wooden doorway he was met with dim light, cigarette smoke and a low hum of noise. He looked around with feigned casual interest, when in truth, he felt appalled. He cleared his throat. "I'd very much like to get a peek at your establishment, and to meet this paragon sister of yours, if you wouldn't mind."

"You want to meet Jillian?"

"Is that a problem?"

"No, it's just...why?"

He shrugged, trying to fetch forth a logical excuse that wouldn't make her more suspicious. *So I can describe her to Dalton.* "Because she's your sister, and I'm vastly curious."

Charlie looked doubtful, but just then the door to Harry's left burst open and a tall, slender, very young girl bounded into the hallway. "Charlie!"

Harry had already thrust Charlie behind him and taken a fighter's stance. The girl's eyes widened as she stopped dead in her tracks, one hand lifting to her throat. From behind him, Charlie snickered in a most irritating way.

And Harry muttered, "Ah, hell."

Peeking from around him, Charlie said, "Harry, meet my sister, Jillian. Sis, this is Harry Lonnigan. You'll have to ignore his chivalry, but you did bust out like a tornado. You see, Harry has these odd heroic tendencies, and he was trying to protect me, in case you were a threat."

Harry pulled her around to the front of him and growled, "I am not a hero."

"No? Well, Ted or the dogs might disagree. And you saved me from a pager today, remember? And now you just protected me from my sister." She snickered again, and the sound grated along his raw nerves. "You're either a hero, or you're nuts. Take your pick."

CHARLIE CONTINUED to smile as Jillian cautiously stepped forward, her eyes huge, staring at Harry with absolute awe. Charlie knew the feeling. It seemed every time she looked at him, he impressed her anew. He was just so...big. And so manly and hard and solid. Despite the fine clothes, the immaculate haircut, Harry Lonnigan had an aura of savagery about him.

She liked it.

Harry reached out and gently took Jill's hand. "Never mind your rather disputatious sister here. She seems to take immense enjoyment in plaguing me for no evident reason." Jillian stared, and Harry added, "It's a pleasure to meet you, Jillian."

Jillian licked her lips, glanced sideways at Charlie, and whispered, "What did he say?"

Charlie laughed. "Who knows? He always talks funny, but it seems to be getting worse as the night goes on. I think he needs to get some sleep and recharge his wits."

Jillian nodded, then turned back to Harry. She clasped his hand with both of hers. "Thank you so much for bringing my sister home safe and sound. She tends to get herself into trouble awfully easy, but from what she told me, she topped herself tonight."

Harry nodded. "Hmm. Her intentions are good, but she appears to be misguided by too much pride and bravado."

"Yep, that's Charlie. I tried to talk her out of doing something so stupid, but—"

"Jill."

Jill smiled. "Would you like to come up for a drink? I was just making some hot chocolate."

"Jillian..."

"Thank you, I'd love to," Harry said, cutting off Charlie's protest. "Hot chocolate sounds like perfection."

Charlie rubbed her head. "Harry, don't you think it's getting kind of late?"

He glanced at his wristwatch. "Very. What time do you close the bar?"

"At two. And as soon as I change, I have to check on things. So really, it'd be better—"

He gave her his back. "Jillian, if you'd like to lead the way, I'll drink my hot chocolate and then head home. Charlie's absolutely correct that it's been a rather full day."

Jill smiled. "Follow me."

Eyes narrowed, Charlie stomped along behind them up the silent stairwell. When they reached the top, Jill used the key hanging from her wrist to unlock the door. She said over her shoulder to Harry, "The doors automatically lock when they shut."

"Good idea. Are you ever bothered by the noise downstairs?"

"Not at all. I'm used to it."

"And the patrons respect your privacy?"

"Patrons?" Jill giggled as she headed down another hall and into the kitchen, the first room on the left at the top of the landing. Water already boiled in a softly whistling teapot, so Charlie got down three mugs and the tin of chocolate powder. Jillian dug three spoons from the drawer. "I'd hardly call the guys who hang out here 'patrons.'"

"No? Then what would you call them?" Harry seated himself at the Formica table and crossed his long legs. He looked entirely too much at his leisure to suit Charlie, especially when she noted him looking around, surveying their small but tidy kitchen.

Jill shrugged. "I don't know. Regulars? I suppose that's the nicest thing I can come up with. Oh, really, they're not all bad. But as Charlie has always told me, we attract a certain clientele here at the Lucky Goose, and it doesn't include anyone who's too discriminating."

Charlie finished stirring in the chocolate and handed Harry his cup. He sipped, made appropriate sounds of approval, then leaned back in his chair. "Do you ever go into the bar?"

"Are you kidding? Charlie has fits if I even peek in there after four o'clock. Before that, it's pretty tame, just a few guys hanging around, usually getting a sandwich and a beer. She doesn't mind if I'm in there then. But the rowdiest crowds don't start until after seven."

"What time do you open?"

"Charlie opens it up from two in the afternoon to two in the morning. She's got things pretty organized and we get a pretty steady crowd."

Harry made a pretense of drinking his chocolate, but Charlie could easily see the crafty interest in his gaze. "Those are long hours to work. What other employees do you have?"

Waving a hand, Jill commented, "Charlie likes to keep things simple, so she doesn't hire in much help. She does almost everything herself, which means she works much more than she should."

"So it seems."

"The only relaxation she gets is in the tub. I swear, she'll soak for hours. There've been a few times she's fallen asleep in there—"

"Jill." Charlie could feel the heat pulsing in her face.

Twin dimples showed in her sister's cheeks when she grinned, proving Charlie's warnings did little good.

"We have a bouncer, of course, who also serves as a bartender on occasion. Then there's the regular bartender, and two women who help serve drinks during the busiest hours. Other than them, we have a few part-timers who fill in every now and then."

"Do you have need of the bouncer very often?"

"Nope." Jill leaned forward and dropped her tone to a conspiratorial whisper. "If you saw the guy Charlie hired, you'd know why. He's a real sweetheart, but no one seems to know that, and given his handicap and the way he always—"

Charlie interrupted, thumping her mug of chocolate onto the table and spilling a bit. "That's enough, Jill." She didn't want Harry getting the idea she had an overly soft heart, but if Jill had her way, she'd start telling stories that could give anyone the wrong impression. Her sister had a way of slanting the perspective to always put Charlie in a very rosy light.

She narrowed her gaze at Harry. "Okay, give. Why the third degree?"

After another long drink of his chocolate, Harry pretended confusion. "I have no idea what you're talking about. I was only making idle chitchat."

"Chitchat? Is that what you call it?" She glanced at Jill, who looked horrified by her sister's sudden rudeness, and explained, "Harry's a P.I. Snooping is his business."

Fascinated, Jill stared.

Harry raised a supercilious eyebrow. "Actually, I investigate. I do not snoop."

"Uh-huh. So why snoop here? I'm paying you to check on my father, not to pry into my personal life."

Jill groaned. "Oh, Charlie, you didn't? I thought we agreed! There's no reason—"

"Don't start being dramatic, Jill." In an aside to

Harry, she explained, "Jill is prone to melodrama, no doubt because of her age."

Harry made a rude sound to that. "More likely due to her sister's penchant to get into trouble."

"Harry—"

"No, don't berate me. My brain is tired and I really do need to head home." He finished off the chocolate, stood, then took Jill's hand once again. "It's amazing your hair is still brown and not gray. I swear, while I was with her today, I could feel the gray hairs struggling to sprout."

Jill giggled. "She has a way about her."

"Indeed."

"She's also the very best sister in the world."

"I got that impression."

"That's enough out of both of you!" Charlie circled the table and stood toe to toe with Harry. She had to bend her head way back to meet his gaze. "When do you think you'll know something?"

He cocked a brow. "I know an abundance of things, Charlie. Can you be more specific?"

She ground her teeth together. "When, exactly, do you think you'll be able to give me some info on my father? I don't mean to rush you, but I don't want to wait too long, either."

"Patience," Jill muttered as she put Harry's mug in the sink, "is not one of Charlie's strong suits."

She was ready to refute that when Harry touched her cheek with two fingers. "I'll get back to you just as soon as I can. Try not to worry, okay?"

She gulped, feeling that simple touch all the way to

her bare toes and back up again. "Can you...maybe give me a ballpark guess?"

He smiled. "I'll tell you what. Give me your phone number and I'll call you tomorrow evening. By then I should be able to have a better idea, okay?"

Charlie hurried to a drawer to pull out a pen and paper. "I'll give you our personal number, for here in the apartment, and the number for the Lucky Goose. You should be able to reach me at one or the other."

Harry slid the slip of paper into his back pocket. "Jill, thank you for the drink."

"Thank you, Harry, for bringing Charlie home in one piece."

"That was my pleasure. Well, at least part of the time. There was the occasional moment when—"

With a shove, Charlie started him on his way. She knew he was laughing, but she didn't mind. She walked him down the stairs and with every step, her heart thumped heavily. She was so acutely aware of him beside her, tall and strong and warm. When they reached the end of the stairwell, Charlie still one step above him, putting her on more even ground, she caught his arm before he could open the door.

He turned to face her, his look questioning.

She cleared her throat. His biceps were large and thick and she knew even both her hands wouldn't circle him completely. She lightly caressed him and her breathing hitched. She was so damn ignorant about this sort of thing. "Harry, I really do appreciate all you did tonight. Not that I couldn't have handled it on my own—"

"But it was nice to have the company? My sentiments exactly."

She tilted her head, searching for the right words. This entire situation was awkward for her, because she'd never really wanted anyone before. "I know you said you don't want to get involved, and I feel the same way."

His entire expression softened. "Charlie—"

"No, you don't need to explain. I understand. But..."

"But what?"

His voice was low, the words gentle. She could feel him looking down at her, and so she mustered her courage, looked him straight in the eye, and said, "But I want you. There. I said it."

He stared, shock plain on his face, and she took advantage of it, throwing herself against him. She felt his arms automatically catch her, and she kissed him while his mouth was still open in surprise. He was motionless only a moment, then he turned, pinned her to the wall, and with a low deep groan, proceeded to kiss her silly.

6

HARRY ENTERED the hospital with his heart in his throat and his pulse racing. The day, which had begun with no indications of a catastrophe, continued to slide rapidly downhill. Actually, he thought, he was well into a new day. Surely things would begin improving, surely Dalton would be all right.

A nurse directed him to the CCU, or coronary care unit, and the name alone made Harry break out in a sweat. *A heart attack,* Dalton had suffered a heart attack. He felt sick with anxiety and throbbing guilt.

It took him mere seconds to reach the right room, and as soon as he was close enough, he could hear Dalton complaining. He increased his pace, rushed into the room, then came to a standstill.

Dalton, pale and obviously agitated, was in a sterile white bed, oxygen hooked up to his nose, other apparatus connected in various places. He fought to sit up while a nurse struggled to keep him still. Harry drew himself up and said, "What is going on here?"

The nurse looked at him with utter and complete relief, then asked hopefully, "Harry Lonnigan?"

"Yes." He stepped forward and nudged her out of the way, giving Dalton a glare. "Be still."

Dalton rested back with a smile.

The nurse heaved a heartfelt sigh of relief. "He

needs to be resting, but he was insistent on seeing you. I told him we'd left a message for you, but when you couldn't be reached, he wanted to get out of bed and try calling you himself—"

"I'm sorry for the delay. The storm knocked out my answering machine and I didn't receive any message." He frowned at Dalton. "I called your house and the housekeeper told me what happened. I got here as quickly as I could."

Dalton gripped his hand. "She contacted me, Harry."

Harry looked down at the man he loved like a father and winced. Dalton was still good-looking at fifty-nine, tall, lean, with only a smidge of gray mixed in with his dark hair. He'd always looked so vital to Harry, but now, he looked shrunken and frail. "Who contacted you?"

"My daughter."

Everything in Harry jolted. His wits jumped about hither and yon, his heart thumped. He cast a quick glance at the nurse, then squeezed Dalton's hand. To the nurse he asked, "Can I speak with you in just a moment? I'd like to be updated—"

She patted Harry's arm. "Get your father settled, then come out. I'll be at the nurses' station. But please—" and she bent a warning look on Dalton "—he needs to be still and calm."

Harry nodded. "I'll see to it. And thank you."

The nurse went out, closing the door behind her. Harry hadn't bothered explaining to her that Dalton wasn't his father. In all the most important ways, he'd been the only father Harry knew.

The room was silent, with an acoustical ceiling and floor, good lighting, and a variety of electrical, suction, and other outlets. Monitors were hooked up to Dalton, and other assorted machinery sat at the ready. Overall, it should have been a distressing sight, but to Harry, it showed the competent level of emergency care available, giving him a sense of security. Dalton wouldn't die. He was well cared for here.

Harry scooted a narrow chair closer to Dalton's bed and seated himself. He had a feeling a lot had happened that he wasn't aware of.

Dalton gave him a shaky smile. "I got a letter from my daughter today. The oldest one, Charlotte." His smile widened. "She's a gutsy little gal. Do you know what she said? She said I owed her a lot of back child support and she wanted to claim it. She said she *would* claim it. What about that?"

Harry winced, both at the name Dalton called his daughter, and the irony of the situation. So Charlie had sent her father a letter. That was likely her reason for being in the store in the first place. She'd been waiting, Harry remembered, peeking out the window on occasion. And Dalton's jewelry store was directly across the street from the grocery. The little witch. Had she hoped to see her father's reaction?

Would she be happy with the results?

He no sooner thought it than he shook off the disturbing notion. Charlie wanted what she considered her due, but she didn't strike him as the type to wish actual harm on anyone. Well, except maybe Floyd.

Dalton cleared his throat. "The girls...they're alone

now. Charlotte told me in the letter that her mother recently passed away."

"I'm sorry, Dalton."

"It was a hell of a shock, reading that letter and knowing in my gut what my girls have gone through. Rose wasn't much when she was around, but she was still their mother. Damn, if only I could have found them."

Harry wondered where to begin, but before he could finish formulating his thoughts, Dalton actually laughed. "Here I was, watching for a sign from you, then that damn letter arrived. I could hardly believe it—liked to stop my heart."

Oh God. "From what your housekeeper told me, it almost did stop your heart."

"Ha! Now that I know I'm this close to getting my girls back, there's no way I'm going to let a little heart trouble stop me."

Harry stared at Dalton, that *ha!* sounding all too familiar. He wondered if Charlie had inherited the blunt expletive from her father.

"No sir," Dalton continued, full of vehemence. "I'm going to make it up to them, everything they missed out on because I wasn't there. But Harry, I still don't know where they are. The letter didn't say. So I was hoping you could..."

Harry decided before he could say anything, he needed all the details on Dalton's condition. He patted the older man's hand, then slowly stood to pace. "Everything will work out, Dalton, you'll see. As soon as I find out about you, we'll talk about the letter and what to do next, okay?"

"Damn right we'll talk about it. It's all I can think about."

"You need to rest, you know, if you want a chance to meet Charli—Charlotte." He barely caught himself, then shook his head. "Promise me you'll sit there quietly until I get back."

Dalton made a face. "What choice do I have? They've got me connected to so many wires, they know if I'm going to burp before I even do it!"

"Good. I like it that way. Now sit tight and I'll be right back."

It took Harry about ten minutes to find out that Dalton had suffered a mild heart attack, although *mild* wasn't really descriptive of the condition. Dalton had evidently suffered some discomfort through the night, including dizziness, but being the stubborn cuss Harry knew him to be, he'd ignored the problems, determined to be at the shop that day to observe Harry's meeting with Floyd and Ralph.

The nurse didn't know what had upset Dalton, only that a customer had called the paramedics when he'd turned deathly pale and grew nauseous. They took an EKG as soon as he reached the hospital, and then had to insist that Dalton not leave when they found evidence of a heart attack. He kept claiming he had important things to do.

Harry had to shake his head. What rotten timing for Dalton.

The nurse explained that a cardiologist on call had been in to see Dalton, and that they would continue monitoring him throughout the night. He had no prior history of problems and was basically a healthy man.

In the morning they'd check his cardiac enzymes and see how his heart rhythm had done through the night, which would tell them more.

Though the nurse was reassuring, Harry still worried. It took him another five minutes to figure out what he wanted to say to Dalton about Charlie, censuring it in his mind so as not to upset him further. Such an awful situation. He could almost be angry at Charlie, except that her life hadn't been an easy one, and she'd obviously been led to believe her father hadn't cared. Under those circumstances, she could hardly be blamed for her actions.

Dalton's face was turned away, staring out a window when Harry returned. He immediately turned to face him, and that damn smile was back on his face. "You need to read the letter, Harry. It's in my pants pocket, over there in the cabinet. Take it home with you for safekeeping."

Harry retrieved the letter and stuck it in his pocket. "I'll take care of the letter, Dalton, don't worry about that. But first I need to tell you something."

Dalton blinked. "Well, damn, I'd forgotten all about Floyd and Ralph and those other idiots. How did it go? You didn't have any trouble with them, did you? I got that damn letter, had the attack and the next thing I knew I was in here and no one would listen to me when I said I had to call you."

"I'm really sorry about that. You know if I'd gotten the message, nothing could have kept me away."

"Of course I know it. That's why I was worried about you when you didn't show up right away."

Harry swallowed hard. "I have to tell you something, Dalton."

"Out with it. I'm not so delicate I'll swoon, you know."

"Well, to come right to the point, I met your daughter today."

Dalton lurched, he was so surprised, and Harry rushed to soothe him. "Settle down now before they throw me out of here."

"But I don't understand! You met her? Where?"

"In the grocery. She was there, evidently waiting to see your reaction to her letter, though I didn't know she'd sent a letter. I didn't...ah, find out she was your daughter until much later."

"This is incredible!"

"Yes, I know." Harry didn't mean to sound facetious, but the whole situation was too ironic. That last kiss that Charlie had forced on him—forced, ha!—had damn near killed him. He'd forgotten himself, and within a heartbeat he'd had her pressed against the stairwell wall, her small hands clutching him, her hips squirming against his, inciting his lust, making him hard. Damn. Even now he gasped with the pleasure of it. Never in his adult years had he been hit by so much uncontrollable lust. He'd tasted Charlie and wanted to go on tasting her, everywhere, all over her small sweet body. He could have spent hours doing just that.

He shook, remembering.

He'd been a hairsbreadth away from taking her right there in the stairwell, and probably would have if a commotion in the bar hadn't jolted him out of his lust-induced stupor.

After that, he'd all but run from her. And she'd actually had the gall to laugh at his predicament.

He shook his head, wondering how he was ever going to be able to handle this absurd situation. A reluctant smile caught him unawares. "She's something else, Dalton. A little bitty thing, barely reaching my shoulder."

"Everyone just barely reaches your shoulder, Harry. You're what we average people call *tall*."

"She's shorter than most, though. But you're right about the guts. Ralph and Floyd tried to intimidate her, but she easily got the best of them. Calling her fearless would be a gross understatement."

Dalton shuddered. "Thank God you were there to keep her safe. If those hoodlums had hurt her..."

Harry had a feeling she might have done just fine on her own. Under no circumstances would he tell Dalton that she'd been dressed as a boy—or that he was the one who'd inadvertently blown her cover.

Dalton drew a slow breath. "When I last saw her, she was nine, missing a few teeth, skinny as a twig, and loved football much more than dolls. Her mother kept her hair cut short so she wouldn't have to spend time working the tangles out. If I remember it right, Charlotte begged her to do the cutting. She was the epitome of the American tomboy. Of course, she's a young lady now, so none of that matters.

"I worked too many long days back then, and I missed out on so much. Then I caught her mother cheating, found out it wasn't even the first time, and when I sued for divorce, the witch ran off with my kids."

Harry left the chair to sit on the side of the bed. He clasped Dalton's shoulder. "You can explain it all to her now, Dalton. She'll understand. From the time I spent with her, I can tell she inherited her father's intelligence."

"Did she mention me at all?"

This was the tough part, but Harry didn't see any way around a few truths. "As a matter of fact, she wanted to hire me to find out more about you."

"No fooling?" Dalton seemed pleased by his daughter's curiosity.

Harry nodded. "I didn't say I already knew you. I wanted to give you the chance to tell her everything yourself."

"Did you...you know, get a feel for what she thinks of me? What her mother might have told her about me?"

Harry hesitated, unsure just how far he could stretch the truth.

"Out with it, Harry." He grinned. "From her note, I'm already assuming she has a healthy chip on her shoulder where I'm concerned. And knowing her mother the way I did, I can easily guess at how she probably lied about me."

Helpless, Harry admitted, "I think that's more the case than not. Charlie seemed under the impression you'd abandoned them."

"Charlie?"

"That's the name she goes by."

"Ridiculous! She has a lovely name."

Harry kept his opinion in check. By his way of thinking, *Charlie* suited her much better than the too reserved *Charlotte*. Of course, Dalton wasn't reacquainted with her, so couldn't yet know that.

"Did she mention Jillian at all?"

Ah, safer ground. "Actually, I met her. It's a long story, and no, get that look out of your eye because I'm not telling it right now. You've had enough excitement for one day."

"Tyrant."

"I promise to fill you in on all the details tomorrow. But as to Jillian, she's a lovely girl. Eighteen now, and the opposite of Charli—Charlotte. Tall, light brown hair. But the same blue eyes."

Dalton's blue eyes crinkled at the corners with a huge smile. "I have an idea, Harry."

Harry rubbed his forehead with a sigh. The past several hours had depleted him sorely. He needed some sleep, he needed something to eat.

He needed Charlie.

His head snapped up with that errant thought, and he coughed. "Dalton, I'm sure if I go to her now and tell her what's happened—"

"No! You can't do that. Why, she might blame herself for my ill health. Finding out the truth, that I didn't leave her, is going to be enough of an adjustment. She'll know her mother lied all along, that she kept us apart out of sheer spite. That'd be tough for any young lady to accept, especially now that Rose is gone and can't admit the truth."

"Dalton, this particular young lady is tougher than shoe leather. Really. I don't think—"

"No. I tell you, it'd be too much. And if she thought

she caused my heart attack—which of course she didn't—"

"Of course not," Harry agreed with wry cynicism.

"—she just might run off again. I can't take that chance, now that I'm so close to being reunited with her. She just might leave without giving me time to explain."

From what Harry knew of Charlie, she wasn't going anywhere without enough money to get her sister started in the college of her choice. The woman could vie with a herd of mules and come out ahead on stubbornness.

"No," Dalton continued, thinking out loud, "a better idea will be if you pretend to work for her."

"What?"

He rubbed his hands together. "You can soften her up for me, Harry. Leave little hints about the past, pretend to uncover clues about how much I do care for her, to let her know I wasn't just another neglectful father. Then she can get accustomed to the idea little by little. When she's ready, you can arrange a meeting between us."

"You want me to lie to the girl?"

Dalton managed a supreme look of affront. "Not blatant lying, no. Just little white lies, for the good of all of us. Besides, you've already lied to her by not admitting you know me, so don't get sanctimonious on me now."

"Dalton, you're not in the best of health. You've had a really rough day and you're not thinking straight." Besides, Harry wasn't at all certain he could maintain a facade of indifference to Charlie. He wanted her, and being around her while resisting her would be an undeserved hell, especially as she seemed determined to seduce him—when she wasn't doing her best to irritate him.

Dalton slammed his fist down on the side of the bed. "I'm thinking just fine!"

His actions reminded Harry so much of Charlie, how she'd slammed her own smaller fist down on his table, he almost grinned. Stubbornness definitely ran through the genes. Charlie had come by her obstinate nature legitimately. "Okay, so you're impervious to health concerns, wise beyond your years and immortal to boot. I still don't think it's a good idea."

Dalton fell back against his pillows, and Harry again noticed how pale, how drawn he looked. He frowned in concern. "Dalton—"

"No, never mind," Dalton sighed in a pathetically weak voice. "I shouldn't have been such a bother. You're already working on the extortion case for me, and heaven knows that's more than I should have asked of you. Though those young punks are idiots, it could still be dangerous."

Harry could attest to that.

"And now this, dragging you into the middle of my personal affairs." He sighed again, closed his eyes, and looked forlorn and dejected. Even knowing it to be a ruse, Harry couldn't stand it.

He came to his feet and propped his hands on his hips. "You don't play the martyr worth a damn, Dalton, so spare me the theatrics."

Dalton peeked one eye open. "I know that tone. It means you're ready to relent. Right?"

"Yes," Harry said, then groaned. "I suppose I have no choice, given you're lying there in a sickbed and you're not above using it to make me toe the line."

Dalton beamed at him. "You're a real hero, Harry. I don't know what I'd do without you."

"I am not a damn hero!" He felt mired in conflicting emotions. Regret, because Charlie was now off-limits and he was honor-bound to keep his hands off her delectable little body and his thoughts away from lascivious ventures.

Anticipation, because despite being off-limits, he'd be seeing her again and her spunk and wit never ceased to amaze and amuse him.

He also felt anxiety, because he had no idea how he'd placate her infatuation with him while still keeping her a discreet arm's length away. She seemed determined to seduce him, given that last scorching kiss, and he'd have to find a way to feign disinterest without hurting her.

It was enough to boggle the mind, and Harry's mind, at present, was already overtaxed and sluggish. "I'm a stooge maybe, but never a hero."

"Yeah, well, right now, you look like an exhausted stooge. Why don't you go on home and get some sleep? My God, it's nearly dawn. And with all this excitement, I'm suddenly pretty tired myself."

Alarmed, Harry started forward, only to have Dalton wave him away. "It's not my heart, son, only my age and the excitement. Honest. We'll talk later and go over what you should tell Charlotte. We need a plan of action."

"You think I might have forgotten all your sterling

qualities? You think I might not be able to make you sound a veritable icon among men?" Harry tsked. "You should know better, Dalton. I'll sing your praises until she cries mercy."

Somber, Dalton took Harry's hand and squeezed it. "I can't tell you how many times I've wished you were my own son."

Harry felt a lump in his throat that could strangle an elephant. "In all the ways that matter most, you're the only father I've ever had. And a damn good one to boot."

Dalton wiped his eyes, then said gruffly, "Aw, get the hell out of here. You look worse than I do."

Harry laughed. "That's saying a lot." On impulse, he leaned down and gave Dalton a hug, then straightened and headed for the door. "I'll be back, but in the meantime, I'm giving my home number, cell phone number and pager number to the nurses in case you need me for anything."

"You sure you don't want to leave your social security number, too?"

"If I thought it necessary, I would." He heard Dalton grumble and had to smile. "I mean it, Dalton. If you need me for anything, even conversation, simply call, all right?"

"Don't rush back just to hold my hand. Take care of business instead. I'd rather know you were seeing to my daughters and protecting my friends. Besides, there's a few cute nurses here willing to keep me company. If you hang around, they'll all be looking at you, instead."

Shaking his head, Harry said, "I'll let you know

what your daughter thinks of my investigative skills. Even she should be duly impressed, given I'll have found out several remarkable things about you within half a day."

"Make me look real good, son."

"No problem. It'll be a piece of cake."

Or so he wanted Dalton to think. He couldn't abide the idea of causing him undue worry, but he knew from experience that nothing with Charlie would be easy, and she'd be the hardest person in the world to impress, especially where Dalton was concerned.

A reluctant grin curved Harry's mouth as he made his way to the nurses' station. *He would have to spend more time with her*. The decision was out of his hands, his motives altruistic and pure...

It would be a struggle to keep his hands to himself, to keep his thoughts on the straight and narrow. Charlie was just so damn...*cute*, in a perky, twisted, Annie Hall kind of way. He couldn't remember ever being so intrigued by a woman.

He wondered what she'd look like in regular clothes, how she'd dress, how she'd wear her hair.

He also wondered how anyone in his right mind could possibly call such a unique, independent, headstrong woman *Charlotte*. Absurd. Charlie suited her far better. He only hoped Dalton would realize that, to avoid any disappointments.

CHARLIE KNOCKED, but when that didn't bring forth a response, she leaned against the buzzer. Judging by the commotion on the other side of the door, at least the dogs were at home. She really wanted Harry to be in, too, so she could share her news. She needed...

Oh, who was she fooling? She simply wanted to see him again, and when such a good excuse presented itself, she couldn't resist. It was almost noon, so Harry surely was up, despite the late night they'd had. She was amazed she'd managed to wait this long.

Keeping one shoulder on the buzzer, she smoothed her hair, then caught herself and dropped her hand. She was not a prissy person and damn if she'd start acting like one now just because she had the temporary hots for a very urbane gentleman with outlandish diction.

Charlie grinned. Actually, she'd sorta grown used to the way he talked. It was smooth on the ears, certainly not something she was used to when the men at her bar tended to slur and used very crude language.

When the door suddenly opened, she was caught with that outrageous grin still on her face. And Harry, all six feet five inches of him, looked disgruntled. He was—she gulped—wet, and wearing only a towel. The dogs were now quiet, peeking around Harry's bare knees.

His eyes narrowed when he saw her. "Perhaps you're not aware of it, but you're leaning on my doorbell."

Charlie, never to be confused with an idiot, widened her eyes and quickly stepped away from the bell. "Oops! I'm sorry. I didn't realize."

Harry stilled, then slowly looked her over. His gaze lingered on her hair, her breasts, then skimmed down to her feet. She stared back. He stood there blocking his doorway, wearing only a towel, clean shaven. Droplets of water clung to the hair on his chest and trickled through the silky line of hair leading from his navel downward. He smelled of delicious male scents that made heat bloom and curl in her belly. She delicately sniffed the air, breathing him in, then sighed.

His voice was gruff when he said, "You certainly look different out of your male apparel."

Charlie glanced down at her slim-fitting, well-worn jeans, her lace-up brown work boots. Donning a soft, cream-colored sweater was as far as she'd been willing to go to try to impress him with her less than apparent femininity. Anything more, anything as ridiculous as a skirt, would have been too obvious. She wasn't altogether certain she even owned a skirt.

Besides, any efforts to make her look more ladylike would have come across as asinine. She just didn't have the heart for it.

Harry reached out and touched her hair, tugging one curl through his fingers. His cheekbones flushed and he whispered, "Like silk. Warm silk."

Charlie wanted to melt. Oh, the man had a way of saying things that hit the pit of her stomach and radiated out to make her shaky and hot and... She sighed again. If he'd wanted her to, she'd have stood there all day letting him play with her hair. But then his fingers touched on her bullet earring and he suddenly stiffened and stepped back.

"Good heavens. Come in before someone sees you."

"Me? You're the one who's nearly naked."

She walked in, thoroughly greeted by the dogs who

went all out by jumping and shaking and appearing happy to see a new face. Harry, however, was already stalking away. He waved vaguely toward the kitchen. "Go make yourself at home and I'll be right back."

Charlie admired the view of his retreating backside. His shoulders were wide, hard, his spine straight, muscles evident all over the place.

She'd have admired the view even more if he'd dropped the towel. "Don't dress on my account!"

"Brat." He galloped up the steps without looking back. She heard a door slam.

Well, well. He certainly was grouchy this afternoon. Charlie slipped off her lightweight jean jacket, laid it over a chair, and went to investigate the kitchen. The dogs followed on her heels and their nails tapped-tapped on the kitchen tile floor as they danced around her.

She wasn't surprised to find coffee just finished brewing. Remembering how Harry had taken his, she fixed his cup as well as her own. Then she spotted Ted, glaring at her from his seat at the table. She shrugged. "Don't mind me. I'll sit way over here. You won't even know I'm around."

Sooner howled, as if he found that hilariously funny.

Harry returned only seconds later wearing suit pants and buttoning up a blue dress shirt with one hand. In the other hand he carried shoes, socks and a tie.

Charlie raised a brow. "What? You didn't trust me alone in your kitchen? Or did you think Ted and I would be brawling? You had to rush back half-dressed?"

He slanted a frown her way and picked up the coffee cup for a healthy sip. "At least allow the caffeine to penetrate my brain cells before you start sniping. I've had very little sleep, certainly not enough to counteract yesterday's adventures." As if by rote he opened the back door and the dogs darted out.

She hadn't gotten much sleep the night before, either. She'd spent most of the evening staring at the ceiling and thinking of that last kiss. She doubted he'd done the same. Maybe he just slept late when he needed to. She, however, didn't have that luxury, not with the bar to run. "Uh, Harry, are you on your way out?"

"As a matter of fact, yes, so perhaps it would be auspicious for you to explain this unexpected visit?"

"Auspicious, huh? All right, don't get red in the face. I found out some info on our villains."

He froze with the cup to his lips, then slowly lowered it. "I assume you're referring to Floyd and Ralph?"

"Aren't they the only villains we know jointly?"

He frowned, took a large drink as if to fortify himself, and she continued.

"They're going to drop in on Pops again today, so I figured I'd follow them when they leave, just to see where they go, and I wondered if you'd want to tag along to keep me company—"

Coffee spewed across the table, making Charlie jump back a good foot. She growled. "Damn it, Harry, you do seem to have a problem with coffee, don't you?"

He thunked the coffee cup down and took two menacing steps toward her. Ted raced past her with a vicious hissing complaint, but since Harry seemed the bigger threat, she didn't dare look away from him. She widened her stance, braced herself and waited.

Through gritted teeth, he said, "You're not to go anywhere near them, Charlie, is that understood?"

She fetched forth her most direct, intimidating look, and must have succeeded, given his stormy expression. "Uh, Harry. You're not trying to give me orders, are you?"

He stepped closer still, until her neck felt like it might cramp from the drastic angle it took to meet his gaze and his breath hit her face with the force of a puffing bull. "Yes," he said succinctly. "I'm giving you an explicit directive to stay the hell away from anything and anyone that has to do with Ralph and Floyd."

He was so close, she couldn't resist, and leaned just a scant inch closer to smell him, her nose almost touching his chest.

Harry leaped back as if burned. "What do you think you're doing?"

"You smell so good, Harry. If I could bottle you, I'd make a fortune."

He flushed, blustered for a moment, then started in frowning again. "You're trying to distract me, damn it."

Actually, distracting him had never entered her mind. Charlie examined her nails. "They kidnapped me, Harry. They threatened me. You can't expect me to just let them get away with that."

"I told you I'd take care of them."

"Terrific. I'll go along to see that you take care of them right. I haven't forgotten you're the one who was too chicken to push Floyd off the truck."

He looked nearly apoplectic. "You bloodthirsty little...it would have killed him! I do believe I can handle things without resorting to murder."

Charlie sniffed. "He's too mean to die. He'd probably have just gotten his hard head bruised a little."

"Charlie." He clasped her shoulders and shook her lightly. "You don't know what you're playing with."

She wanted to play with him, but he didn't look overly receptive to the idea at the moment. No, he looked like it took all his restraint not to choke her.

"Forget it, Harry. If you're too much a sissy to go with me, I can go alone. No problem."

Choking became a distinct possibility.

After several moments where she held her breath, waiting to see which way the chips would fall, Harry finally released her and stepped away. He picked up his coffee.

She eyed it warily. "Careful. I don't want you to drown yourself."

He drank the rest of the cup in one long swallow, glaring at her over the rim all the while. After he finished the cup, his expression grew crafty. "I have a deal for you, Charlie."

"I'm listening."

"Remove yourself from my business with Floyd

and Ralph, and I'll tell you what I've discovered concerning your father."

Her breath left her in a whoosh and she gripped the edge of the table. "You've found out something already?"

He looked down his nose at her. "Quite a few somethings, actually, which is why I didn't get to bed until the early hours of the morning, and why I was just rising when you arrived. Now, do we have a deal or not?"

Charlie weighed her options, decided lying would be the most expedient way to go, and said, "Whatever you say, Harry. Now tell me everything you know."

7

HARRY STARED AT her hard, but she didn't so much as flinch. Still, he knew without a shadow of a doubt she had no intention of backing away from Ralph and Floyd, despite her rapid agreement.

With a sound of disgust, he dropped into a chair and bent to pull on his socks. "You're lying through your teeth and you aren't even doing it well."

"That's absurd!" She pulled out a chair and sprawled into it. "I'm an *excellent* liar!"

He looked nonplussed for a moment, then laughed. "You're something else, you know that, Charlie?"

He sounded...affectionately exasperated. But then what did she know? She'd never heard honest affection from a man before. And she'd certainly never known a man like Harry. "I like watching you dress, Harry." He glanced up at her, startled, and she smiled. "I think I'd probably like watching you undress, more."

A shoe dropped from his hand, thumping onto the floor. Harry swallowed, made a strangled sound. Charlie eyed him. "Thank God you're not drinking coffee, huh?"

He stared, then jerked his gaze away from her. Furious, he yanked on the rest of his clothes, including a silk tie, then began pacing the kitchen. Glancing at her, he accused, "You've traumatized my cat."

"I'm not the one who can't swallow coffee."

His eyes narrowed. He looked downright harassed, and he kept checking his watch. The dogs scratched to come in, and again he went through the chore of cleaning their feet. Afterward, the dogs cuddled up to him and got thoroughly petted. He even whispered to them, though she couldn't hear what he said.

Charlie loved watching him with the animals. He was so big, so strong, but so incredibly gentle, too. She remembered the way he'd touched her, how he'd kissed her, and she was instantly jealous of the attention he lavished on his pets.

When Harry stood, Sooner and Grace came over to her for a few pats. Harry watched, his brows down, and he warned, "Don't try to ingratiate yourself with my dogs. I already explained to them how conniving you can be."

She gave each dog an extra hug. "Yeah, well, since they know you, they've probably realized you're just being unreasonable." The dogs didn't agree or disagree, they just went off to sleep.

Charlie crossed her legs and waited. He had news to tell her, but she did her best to look indifferent despite the churning in her belly and her anxiety. She couldn't give him the upper hand.

"Okay, are you interested in knowing what I've discovered or not?"

"What a dumb question! Of course I'm interested." Then in the coolest tone she could manage, she asked,

"Do you think he has any money? Will he be able to pay what he owes?"

Charlie watched, fascinated, as Harry's lean jaw hardened, as his muscles bunched and flexed. For a second there she thought his eyes turned red, but then he stepped around her and headed out of the kitchen.

"We'll have to discuss this in transit. I'm late already."

Charlie hustled after him. "Late for what?"

The look he gave her wasn't promising. "I was intending to tail Floyd and Ralph."

Grinning, she skipped to keep up with his long-legged stride. "Then you already knew—"

He held her jean jacket while she slipped it back on, causing her thoughts to jumble. It was a first for her, that small courtesy, and it amused her that even while he was so obviously irritated with her, his unrelenting manners came through.

She leaned back against him as he settled the coat over her shoulders, and he jumped away, grumbling, cautioning her "Charlie...".

"Hmm?"

He frowned, blinked at her, then shook his head. "Come on, let's get going."

Charlie had to hide a smile. He fought her, but he was tempted. Maybe she'd be able to work on that.

Looking decidedly perturbed, Harry pulled on a suit coat, then his raincoat. The dogs stirred themselves enough to look up as Harry said goodbye to them, then they went back to sleeping peacefully. He led her out the door, locking it behind him.

"So, Harry, you did know about the visit Ralph and Floyd have planned?"

"Of course I knew. I'm the P.I., if you'll recall."

"Well, I only found out late last night from a regular. When I went in to close the bar, I overheard two guys talking and I recognized part of what they said. I asked a few questions and found out Ralph and Floyd have been trying to drum up some assistance."

Harry led her to his car and opened her door. "You shouldn't be asking questions, Charlie. What if it gets back to Ralph or Floyd and they figure out where you live? Is that what you want?"

"Of course not. I'm not an idiot, I know what to say and not say. I was careful."

"You don't know the meaning of the word *careful*." He looked at her long and hard, then touched her cheek. "I don't want to have to worry about you."

Contentment bubbled up inside her. "I don't want to worry about you either, Harry. That's why I thought it'd be nice if we did this together. I mean, considering you're so squeamish about actually hurting anyone." And it'd give her a good excuse to spend more time alone with him.

He dropped his hand and sighed. "Get in the car, Charlie."

"I brought my own transportation. Will you drive me back here?" She'd almost taken the bus today, then realized leaving her truck behind would provide a good excuse to return to his apartment. Her plans weren't exactly orthodox, but then, neither was she.

Her life had never been easy, and she'd learned to be hard and brazen and forceful by necessity, to take

care of her mother, to protect her sister. Now, for the
first time that she could ever remember, she really
wanted a man. She didn't know how to deal with that
except to give it her best shot.

Harry rubbed the back of his neck, cursed softly,
then asked, "I don't suppose you'll go on home and let
me take care of things?"

"Ha! Don't be stupid, Harry."

"No, I didn't think so. All right, yes. I'll bring you
back here. But Charlie, promise me you'll do as I tell
you. I don't want to drag you along only so you can
act recklessly again and end up hurt."

She slid into the stupendous car with the butter-soft
leather seats and the smell of money. "I'm never reck-
less. Quit worrying. You're starting to sound like Jill."

He slammed her car door.

They were five minutes on the road before Charlie
said, "All right. Are you waiting for me to beg or
what?"

He glanced at her, clearly distracted.

"Harry, what did you find out about my father?"

"Oh, sorry. My mind wandered."

"Where did it wander to?"

He stared hard at the road. "Never mind. Besides,
you seemed so disinterested, I wasn't sure you even
cared."

She scooted closer to him. "Didn't you sleep well,
Harry? You're awfully snide today."

"I slept fine for the short time I had in bed."

Very casually, she touched his thigh. It was hard
and warm and the muscles flinched under her palm.
She smiled. "Now who's lying?"

He growled, gripped the wheel, then blurted, "By all accounts, your father didn't abandon you."

That was *not* what she'd been expecting to hear. She was so surprised, she sat back on her own side of the seat, releasing Harry. The old resentment rose to the surface, and her tone was sharper than she intended when she said, "No? He had amnesia and forgot he had children? He was taken prisoner in a foreign country and only just got free? It's been eighteen years since I've seen him or heard from him, Harry. I'd pretty much call that abandoned."

Harry sighed, then incredibly, reached for her hand. "Honey, he tried to find you. He really did."

He called her *honey*. She felt all warm and mushy inside again. Clearing her throat, she asked, "How do you know that?"

"He's worked at that same jewelry store for some time now, so a lot of the other proprietors are familiar with him. Many of them told me he's spent years looking for his daughters, that even now he hasn't given up hope of finding you."

She tried to pull her hand away, but he held her tight. "Charlie, he cares about you and Jill."

Charlie swallowed down the unfamiliar lump of emotion in her throat. Even if what he said was true, it didn't matter. "Concern and caring from a father back when I...I had to work two jobs and my mother was so sick and Jill got cheated out of Christmas twice would have been real nice. But I don't care anymore about that. All I want from him now is enough money to get Jill through college. Does he have money, Harry?"

Harry sighed, and she snapped, "Oh, stop that!

You're forever sighing, like you're so put-upon whenever we're together."

He fought a smile. "I'm sorry. I suppose it's just that I expected that answer from you, and I'll admit I'm disappointed. Charlie, your father can't help it if your mother took off and he couldn't find you."

She snorted. "How hard did he try? True, we moved around a lot. I remember that, mostly because it made it so damn difficult for me to get Jill settled. But even so, a single woman with two children should be easy enough to track down. The school records alone—"

"Did you go to public schools?"

"Yeah, well...come to think of it, we almost always settled in real small towns."

"How small?"

She forced a casual shrug. "Almost nonexistent. The schools were independently run by the townsfolk, since there usually wasn't more than a handful of kids attending." She felt a twinge of doubt, but ruthlessly shoved it aside. She would not be suckered that easily. Dalton Jones had a lot to account for. "We chose small towns because the housing was generally cheaper, not because it was a good way to hide!" She hated her own feelings of defensiveness, and added, "It made finding an after-school job almost impossible. At least, until I got older."

His large thumb brushed over her knuckles, gently, soothing. "Where did you work, Charlie?"

She stared at their linked hands and marvelled that such a simple touch could make her feel so funny. Funny in a very *nice* way. "When I was twelve, I got a job helping out at a market stand. It was seasonal, but I loved it. Being outside, meeting so many people. And I didn't have to dress up. In one town, my mom got me a job helping this old lady out at her boutique. I hated it. She expected me to wear dresses."

Harry laughed. "You're not into female frippery?"

"Can you imagine me in a dress, Harry? It's ridiculous." She stupidly blushed just thinking about it. But whenever she talked about that time of her life, she felt vulnerable. She'd been out of her element, and it had been the first time she'd realized just how different she was, and what a disappointment she was to her mother.

He sobered, then pulled up to a red light. "I think you'd look very nice in a dress, but no more so than you do in those snug jeans."

Her heartbeat tripped. "You...uh, like my jeans?"

He kept his gaze deliberately on the road. "You're very attractive, Charlie, regardless of what you're wearing. Surely men tell you that often?"

She wrinkled her nose. "I work in a bar, Harry. Men tell me a lot of things, but I don't pay much attention to slurred words and suggestive innuendo."

"Will you pay attention to me?"

She felt flushed and drew a slow deep breath. "Since you haven't been drinking all day, and your words are coherent, then sure. I suppose so."

He looked undecided for a moment, then turned to face her. "You're beautiful." Their gazes locked, and Charlie felt drawn in, surrounded by his attention. His hand released hers, but then lifted to her cheek. He smoothed the back of his knuckles over her cheekbone in a very tender gesture, tucked a curl behind her ear. She could get very used to being touched so tenderly. "You don't need any frills to turn a man on, Charlie."

"Really?"

He continued to touch her, small touches that elicited so many feelings. "I think you're one of the sexiest women I've ever met."

"Then..."

"But I'm not going to get involved with you. It has nothing to do with you, and everything to do with me. Okay?"

"No."

"Charlie—"

She laughed, because he looked so frustrated. She decided a dose of honesty couldn't hurt. "I want you, Harry. That's pretty unique for me, so I can't just forget about it. Besides, I'm used to fighting for what I want." When his eyes nearly crossed, she said, "Go ahead and sigh if you really need to, but it won't change anything. Consider yourself forewarned."

A horn blared, prompting Harry to drive now that the light was green. He shook his head, then chuckled as he stepped on the gas. "Only you, Charlie, could make a seduction sound like a threat."

She lifted her nose and tried for a seductive look. He didn't laugh, so she considered herself more successful than not. "I prefer to think of it as a promise, Harry."

HARRY FELT strung too tight. It was absolute torture, sitting next to Charlie while knowing she was smugly plotting his salacious downfall. He could tell by the

way her dark blue eyes slanted in his direction every
so often, or the way she looked him over, as if sizing
him up for a meal. It was possibly the most erotic
thing that had ever happened to him.

And he couldn't do a damn thing about it.

He shouldn't have shored up her confidence by admitting he found her sexy. But he couldn't help himself. The second she started speaking of her past, she'd
looked...uncertain, not her normal indomitable self.
Her eyes, usually so forthright, had filled with reserve
and he'd wanted nothing more than to reassure her.

Now she knew he was susceptible to her, and he
could almost hear the wheels turning in her head.

He needed a distraction, but he was hesitant to pursue the topic of her father. Maybe after she considered
things, she'd soften just a bit. She was bullheaded, but
not cruel. He decided on the next order of business.
"Are you at all nervous about seeing Ralph or Floyd
again?"

She gave him a double take. "Nervous?"

"Yes. It would make sense, you know. Yesterday
was fairly tempestuous, what with being kidnapped
and held at gunpoint."

Strangely enough, her expression softened. "We
were shot at, too."

"Yes."

Suddenly she scooted closer and hugged herself up
to his right arm. "Harry, I think it's wonderful that
you're still determined to protect those old people despite being scared."

"*What?*"

"It's nothing to be ashamed of. As you said, yesterday wasn't easy. It even rattled me a little."

"Well, gee. That makes me feel so much better."

She patted his shoulder. Then rubbed. Then squeezed. "You have very nice muscles, Harry."

"Stop that!" Her voice had gone all throaty and warm. "Return to your own seat and put on your seat belt."

"Sheesh. I was only trying to—"

"Comfort me? This may come as a shock to you, Charlie, but I wasn't unduly upset by what happened. I was, in fact, mostly just concerned for you."

"What? Now why would you be worried about me?"

"Why, indeed?"

Her lip curled and she gave him a look fraught with disgust. "Because I'm *female?*"

Hiding a smile, he added, "And small. It's the truth, honey, you're on the...short side."

She stretched out her spine, managing to look an inch taller. "What the hell does that have to do with anything?"

Now she looked more inclined to punch him than kiss him. He felt relief—and other things he didn't even want to ponder. "My wife was a small woman. Not as small as you, but still considered petite. She hated it that I chose to be a P.I. In fact, she flatly refused to have anything to do with it."

"How could she be married to an investigator and not have anything to do with it?"

"Ah. Good question."

"Oh, you're divorced." She winced. "Is that the reason you broke up? Just because of what you do?"

"I had other options. My father had recently passed away and he'd left me a small fortune, as well as the opportunity to get involved in his business ventures. But I had no interest in such things." He lifted one brow. "She was adamant that I toe the line, that I give in to her will, but as it turns out...I didn't. And she couldn't stand it. She said my job was too dangerous, and if I didn't give it up, she'd leave me."

"And she did?"

He nodded. "Without much reluctance, but with a lot of dissension. She's remarried now, very happily. And she controls her husband with a velvet glove."

"I think your job could be exciting, although so far it's been kind of dull."

"Is that so?"

"And Harry? I don't own any velvet gloves."

He glanced at her, then grinned. "I wasn't drawing a comparison, brat. Well, perhaps I was, in an obscure, peripheral manner. You may not own velvet gloves, but I'll bet you own leather ones—maybe boxing gloves. Or possibly even brass knuckles?"

She blushed, giving herself away. "One of the men at the bar had a pair of those. I confiscated them when he kept causing trouble."

Harry raised a brow, wondering exactly how she'd accomplished that. "You're unlike her in many ways, Charlie. But you're even more controlling." It dawned on him that he could use this argument to turn her away from her seductive course. He truly had no intention of getting involved with any woman who wanted to call the shots.

"Harry, this may come as a shock, but I didn't ask for your hand in marriage. I just want to try out this...um..."

Knowing Charlie and her penchant for boldness, he decided to help her out before she said something too descriptive, too luring, that would push him right over the edge. He cleared his throat and offered, "Chemistry?"

"Yeah!" She beamed at him. "This chemistry we have going. I like it. I've never felt it before."

He gulped and almost swerved off the road. He shouldn't ask, because the less he knew, the better, but he couldn't seem to keep the words contained. He *had* to know. "Never, as in...?"

"As in never. The men I've known weren't the type to inspire illusions of lust. It's the truth, and I hope you won't hold it against me, but I'm pretty much inexperienced in this kind of thing."

He closed his eyes briefly, not enough to wreck his car, but enough to suffer a moment of silence. When he opened them again, he realized nothing had changed. He still could barely breathe. How did she keep doing this to him? "Charlie, when you say inexperienced, do you mean—"

"I'm almost a virgin."

His head throbbed. "How does a woman remain *almost* a virgin?"

She shrugged. "Once when I was nineteen, I felt rebellious and gave in to this total dweeb who lived close to us. What a mistake that was! I ended up punching him in the nose he was so inept. I mean, I *was* a virgin then, and he was twenty-two years old, and supposedly experienced, but even I knew more than he did. And he was so obnoxious about it, blaming me." She snorted in renewed righteous indignation over the slight.

"Good God."

"Then, when I was twenty-three, I got engaged to a guy I thought was nice. And even though I didn't really want him particularly bad, I figured I should know if we were compatible in bed or not before I shackled myself to him."

"And?"

"It's a good thing I didn't marry him." She shuddered in revulsion, then twisted in the seat to face Harry, full of confidences. In a stage whisper, she said, "He peeled off his clothes, and Harry, he had hickeys that I hadn't given to him in the strangest damn places!"

Harry bit his lip.

"Ooh, it was disgusting." Her voice lowered even more. "And his body wasn't all that great, either. Nothing like yours. He didn't have any hair at all on his chest. Slick as a baby's bottom. Can you imagine?"

Harry, who had a nice covering of chest hair, sighed. Well, hell. "You know, you really could benefit from just a pinch of discretion."

"I shouldn't have told you?"

"I might have suffered less not knowing." Her admiration had the ability to fully arouse him from one heartbeat to the next. He could already envision her fingers tangled in his chest hair, smoothing, stroking...

"Why should you suffer? I'm the one who's had to contend with fools and abstinence."

He choked on a laugh. "Charlie—"

In a mournful tone worthy of the divine, she said, "It really has been rough, you know."

Dalton's daughter, Dalton's daughter, Dalton's...

She peeked up at him, a study of feminine adoration. "If he'd looked anything like you, Harry, I might have been able to ignore the hickeys, even though they weren't mine, and even though I can't imagine anyone putting their mouth on him *there.* But he wasn't you and he'd been with someone else. And if I wasn't going to marry him, and of course, after knowing that, I wasn't, then I didn't think I should have to sleep with him."

Harry didn't think she should have to, either. He didn't particularly want to think of her sleeping with anyone, certainly not a man with a hairless chest, not a man who'd been with someone else and gotten love bites in unlikely places. *What places?* No, he didn't care what places. He didn't want her with any man, except maybe himself, and he was out of bounds.

He pulled up to the curb across the street and a few doors down from where their human targets would be making mischief. "Promise me that no matter what, you'll keep your cute little bottom in my car. I don't want you to start—"

"You think my bottom is cute?"

He bit his tongue. "It's a figure of speech used whenever addressing female bottoms."

"Oh."

"Promise me."

She shrugged. "I don't intend to start a brawl in the middle of the street, if that's what you're worried about."

"You're unpredictable. I worry about a lot of things." He glanced at his wristwatch. "We have some time before our neighborhood psychopaths are due to exit. There's a pattern to their visits, and they have the timing down. It's my hope to do nothing more than follow them today, see where they go, then perhaps I can turn the authorities on them without involving the proprietors."

"Why don't the proprietors want to be involved?"

"They want to be involved. Badly. If it was left up to them, they'd have set a trap already and, like vigilantes, exacted their own sort of justice, which I have a feeling is as bloodthirsty as your own. But my...friend, fears retribution against them if they do so. Being the stubborn cusses they are, they refuse to involve the police. They've called on them a few times, for less serious issues—minor vandalism, loud music, loitering, that sort of thing. And the police were unable to do much more than offer to drive by more frequently. It injured their pride."

"And so they've given up on the police?"

Harry nodded. "I can understand them. They're older, but resistant to the idea of being frail. All their lives they've been independent, able to handle all situations. They're settled and productive and happy. Then a few months ago the extortion began, and they can't tolerate it, but their pride insists they don't need the police now, not when they couldn't help them in the past. My friend is concerned, of course, but he did promise them he wouldn't contact the law. And actually, I'm concerned that if they did, especially without rock solid evidence, things could become worse. Ralph and Floyd are only minions. They answer to Carlyle."

"So it's Carlyle you want?"

"Yes, I want him. Badly." Harry rubbed his hands together, imagining what he'd do to Carlyle. "I detest a bully, but a bully who picks on the elderly ranks right up there with the devil himself. With any luck, once I find out where they gather, I'll be able to link them with more than extortion. They're criminals, and I hope to find them with illegal firearms, drugs, anything that will implicate them with the law, without involving the extortion."

He happened to glance over at Charlie, and caught her staring—worshipful lust in her big blue eyes. He scowled. "Stop that."

Her smile was almost sappy. "You're incredible, Harry. A real—"

"Don't say it!"

"But don't you see? You are a hero."

He bent a severe, utterly serious look on her, determined to make her back off before his control snapped. "I'm not a damn white knight, Charlie. I'm not the man you've been waiting for, even though I have a hairy chest and no unseemly love bites. I'm doing a job, that's all."

"I saw the way you looked, how eager you are to get hold of Carlyle. You're a good man, Harry. And good men are few and far between. Believe me, I know."

She looked warm and soft and admiring, and he liked it. He responded to it. She was such an enigma, so strong, so outspoken and confident, yet still so very female. She was quirky, rough around the edges, but so brutally honest she took his breath away. And unlike his ex-wife, she seemed to thrive on the excitement of his job. She actually admired him for what he did, rather than disdaining his choices.

Of course, she also thought he was afraid, and as much as that rankled, he supposed allowing her to believe in some flaws would only add to his efforts to push her away.

He clenched his muscles and forced his honor to the forefront of his brain, nudging the lust aside. "Your father is a good man, by all accounts." She stiffened immediately, but he pressed on. "Wouldn't you like to meet him? I could arrange it, you know."

"That's not necessary."

"You should be pleased, Charlie," he said gently, knowing this was difficult for her, glimpsing again that damn vulnerability that squeezed his heart. "He can assist you financially, and he can be a friend, if you'll let him."

He saw it in her eyes before she even moved. The determination, the cunning. He braced himself, both distressed and anxious, and then she was against him, her hands gripping his shoulders, her body as close as she could get it.

"I don't need a friend, Harry. Right now, I need a lover. You." She kissed him.

Harry tried to resist, he really did. But as he kept telling people, he was far from a hero. Mortal men couldn't be expected to withstand such provocation. He made a desperate effort to recite all the reasons he shouldn't kiss her back; it didn't work.

He felt her breath on his jaw, the silkiness of her hair on his temple when she slanted her head. Her tongue stroked tentatively over his closed lips and he groaned.

"Harry, please..."

Before he knew it, his hands were on her body, under her blue-jean jacket, cupping her small, perfect breasts through her sweater, and there was nothing mysterious about them. They were soft and firm and her nipples burned against his palms. *"Damn."*

Charlie panted. She bit his jaw, nuzzled his neck and kissed his throat. Somehow she managed to get one slender thigh up and over his and he helped her, smoothing a hand over that luscious, resilient bottom and cuddling her closer, letting his fingers probe and explore and entice. She straddled his lap and he could feel her feminine heat from the juncture of her thighs against his abdomen, and it made him nearly wild with need. He wanted her naked, in this same position, riding him gently, then not so gently. He groaned.

With her breasts pressed to his chest, her heartbeat mimicked the furious rhythm of his own.

Then he heard a shout.

He opened his eyes, trying to orient himself and his fogged brain. He saw Floyd scurry out of the meat market, his last stop of the day. Harry stiffened.

Ralph had already gotten in on the passenger's side

of a blue sedan, and two seconds later, just as Floyd got the driver's door open, the proprietor, Moses, came out swinging a fist.

All hell broke loose.

8

CHARLIE WAS shocked when Harry suddenly tossed her into her own seat with the growled order to buckle her seat belt. The convertible ripped away from the curb, leaving the smell of burnt rubber in the air and a number of interested folks on the sidewalk. Charlie managed to say, "What the hell—" before Harry grabbed her head and forced it down in the seat.

"Stay down."

Furious and confused, she tried to lift back up, but his hand remained locked in her hair, keeping her immobile. She thought about punching him, but the car was going too fast, swerving, then pulling away again with a vicious squeal of tires. Harry released her, using both hands to turn the wheel sharply, and when she sat up, more than a little ready to commit murder, she found he had a look of grim satisfaction on his face.

Charlie huffed. Her body was still tingling all over, her mind sluggish, her heart beating too fast. As she smoothed her hair out of her eyes, she decided to give him a chance to explain before she extracted revenge for his high-handedness. "You care to tell me what that macho display was about?"

He cast her a quick glance, then brought his gaze

back to the road. "We're distracting Floyd, before he hits Moses and I have to kill him."

"Moses?"

Harry nodded while constantly glancing in the rearview mirror. They were doing about seventy-five and still gaining speed. "A grouchy old relic who's evidently gotten tired of being robbed. His shop is part of the lineup Floyd hits. Moses took a swing at Floyd as they left the store, but when I cut close to him, he leaped out of the way and forgot about retaliating in favor of trying to catch us."

Excitement bubbled up inside her. She whipped around and sure enough, there was a blue sedan trailing right behind them. "Does he know it's us?"

"I have no idea. Not that it matters. Hold on."

She barely had time to grip the door handle before the car took a sharp turn onto a side street, without slowing down much at all. Charlie fetched up against the door, then just as quickly found herself thrown against Harry.

"I told you to hold on!"

"I'm trying!" Readjusting her position, she again looked out back. "I don't see him."

"That was the point. Now that we've lost him, we'll circle back around and still be able to follow him."

"That won't be risky?"

His lips firmed in a calculating smile. "Are you getting nervous on me, Charlie?"

He sounded downright hopeful and she scowled. "No way. I just want to know what we're doing."

"I'm tracking. You're just along for the ride." The car slowed a tiny bit as Harry maneuvered in and out of side streets. "And this is the last time. I work much better alone."

"Suit yourself. I can work alone, too."

He growled, surprising her with the suddenness of it. "You're not going to work on this, Charlie. Promise me, or I'll pull over right now and toss you out."

He sounded serious, but she didn't think he'd actually do it. He'd lose too much time in trying to catch up with the Bumbling Boys. "Go ahead. I can make my own way home, or rather, back to your place. Then I'll get my truck and start my own surveillance."

Whatever he said was mumbled low enough that she couldn't hear, but his inflection was plain enough. He was beyond frustrated and likely wishing a curse on her head. Then his expression sharpened and a slow smile appeared. "There he is."

Charlie realized with a start that he was enjoying himself. It amazed her that someone so polished could have such an evil smile. Harry pulled into the main flow of traffic, now going a moderate speed that wouldn't draw attention. Charlie looked around, but didn't see a single familiar thing. "Where?"

"About twelve cars up, enough that he probably won't notice us."

"Probably?"

His look was smug. "Even if he does, my car could outrun his any day."

Ah-ha. So there was a reason for the expensive wheels, besides great looks and the expression of wealth. "There's a wild side to you, Harry Lonnigan."

He didn't bother to answer, and she used the quiet moment to study his profile. That last kiss had filled her with unfamiliar tension that still throbbed and teased and kept her edgy. When she'd climbed over his lap, being deliberately brazen in her efforts to seduce him, she'd felt his erection and it had thrilled her.

She smiled, then tilted her head and asked, "Did you like kissing me before?"

His jaw flexed, but he didn't look at her. "Any red-blooded male would enjoy kissing you. It didn't mean anything."

"Because I'm too bossy, like your ex-wife?"

"That's part of it. And no, I'm not up to a barrage of questions right now. Let me concentrate, will you?"

A few minutes later they entered a commercial district where old and new warehouses stood together. Harry slowed the car even more, and eventually pulled up behind an abandoned building. He checked his watch, cursed, then turned to look at Charlie. He chewed his upper lip a moment, his expression both weary and considering. Eyes narrowed, he asked, "Do you think you could handle my car?"

It was the kind of question that never failed to rile her because it pricked her pride. Her spine stiffened and she said, "I can drive anything, including a semi."

"I'm sure that accomplishment will look sterling on a résumé." He held up a hand when she would have replied, and only the seriousness in his gaze kept her from being insulted. "I'm going to go take a look at where our thugs are headed. I'd like you to slide behind the wheel. If anything strange happens, if anyone approaches you, just drive away."

She tucked in her chin and stared at him in disbelief. "Without you?"

"I'll be fine. But not if I have to worry about Floyd getting hold of you again. Believe me, honey, he won't take any chances with you the next time. And his interest isn't only in revenge."

She really liked it when he called her honey. "You think because of my disguise, he's as interested in my breasts as you were?"

Harry drew in a quick breath. His gaze darted to her chest, and then quickly away. His hands tightened on the wheel and he looked ready to snap it in two. "It's possible, but I don't think you'll enjoy his interest."

He looked so furious, she decided against baiting him further. Though she had absolutely no intention of going anywhere without him, she nodded agreement. "Fine."

He studied her face, looking for the deception, but as she'd told him, she was a good liar. He spared her one brisk nod. "Lock the doors as soon as I get out. I should be back in a few minutes. If it takes me more than that, leave."

Then he leaned forward and cupped her chin. Charlie held her breath, hoping for a kiss, but all she got was a threat. "No matter what, don't you dare get out of this car. Do you understand me?"

She especially loved it when he touched her. His hands were always hot, a little rough, and it excited her. She probably would have agreed to anything when he was touching her. She forced air into her lungs and whispered, "I understand."

His gaze dropped to her mouth, and with a slight curse, he pushed himself away. He was out of the car in the next instant. She watched him crouch low and race around the building, keeping to the shadows. More than anything, she wanted to follow him, to protect him, but what if they got separated and he came back to the car? What if Floyd chased him, but she wasn't where she was supposed to be? Though he expected her to run like a coward, she knew Harry would never leave without her. He was naturally protective of anyone or anything smaller than himself. He wanted to help the senior proprietors, he'd willingly tried to shield her from Ralph and Floyd before he'd even known her. And just seeing him with his animals, the way he took care of them, even surly Ted the cat, reaffirmed in her own mind how special Harry was. He could deny it all he wanted, but he had the makings of a true hero.

Waiting was one of the hardest things she'd ever done.

It seemed an hour had passed, but she'd checked the car's clock every minute, and knew it had been less than a quarter of that time. When she saw a shadow fall across the pavement, coming from the direction Harry had disappeared, her shoulders started to sag in relief.

Then the man stepped around the brick building and he looked as shocked to see her as she was to see him. He wasn't Harry, no, not even close. This man was shorter, heavier, and he had an aura of menace about him. Even when he smiled, she wasn't encouraged, because there was no comfort in his baring of teeth or the tilt of his thin lips. Charlie felt her senses scream an alert.

Where the hell was Harry?

The car was still idling, so she put it in gear, undecided on what to do. The man approached as if driven by mere curiosity. He tapped on the window, and Charlie, nervous but not wanting him to know it, lowered the window a scant inch.

The man looked her over. "Is everything okay, miss?"

"Fine, thank you."

She started to roll the window back up, and he quickly asked, "Can I help you with something? This isn't a good place for you to be loitering around alone. Or are you alone?"

She tried to think, but her worry for Harry had doubled and she didn't know what to say. "I'm just...lost."

"Where did you want to be?"

"Um..." Where? She had no idea. She hadn't even been paying that much attention while Harry drove, choosing instead to look at him.

The man grinned again, one brow lifted. "If you'll just roll this window down a little more so we can talk—"

Of course she had no intention of doing any such thing, but then it became a moot point anyway. The man suddenly swung around, but not in time. Harry, who'd crept up with neither she nor the man knowing it, landed a powerful blow against the man's jaw, driving him hard against the car. Charlie jumped.

But the man didn't stay put. In half a heartbeat, he'd pulled himself together and lunged at Harry. Charlie stuck the car in park and would have gotten out to help, but the two men again fell against the car, blocking her door. She tried to climb over the seat and keep watching at the same time. The shorter man hit Harry in the eye, making him curse and duck, then grabbed up a piece of pipe lying on the ground and swung it at Harry's head.

Frozen in very real fear, Charlie screamed.

She struggled with the door, but she'd forgotten it was locked, and by the time her frantic hands got it unlocked and open, Harry was there, cursing her and shoving her back in. "Damn it, I told you to leave!" he roared, and then he slid in beside her, forcing her to move, to climb over the controls to the passenger side while she tried to assure herself his head was still where it was supposed to be.

"Oh my God, are you hurt?"

Harry pushed her away, jerked the car into reverse and stepped on the gas. The car shot backward, and Harry jerked the wheel, spinning the car in one fluid motion so it faced forward, then speeding out of the lot.

Charlie came to her knees beside him and touched the swelling bruise already visible around his eye. "Harry—"

"Put your seat belt on, damn it."

She ignored him. "What happened? I...I thought he was going to hit you with that pipe and—"

"And you screamed." He looked at her, his injured eye swollen almost closed. "I never thought to hear such a female sound from you."

That gave her pause, but she shook the discomfort off. "You weren't even looking. I thought he was going to split your head open."

Harry grunted. "I kicked it out of his hand. The fellow was a totally pathetic fighter, slow and inept, and I'll thank you to have a little more faith in me, if you please."

Charlie sank back on her heels, nonplussed. He was actually insulted that she'd worried for him? "You, ah, handled that very well."

"You didn't." Without looking at her, he began the same tedious drive in and out of side streets, making it difficult for anyone to follow, though he didn't seem overly concerned with the prospect. "I think I could be happy if even once you'd follow my instructions. What were you waiting for? For him to open the car window with the pipe he tried to use on my head? What would you have done if I hadn't shown up?"

"I don't know. But it was dumb of you to tell me to leave without you. I'd never do that."

In a burst of temper, Harry hit the steering wheel with a fist. "This is exactly why you should have kept your stubborn hide at home instead of dogging my heels!"

His tone was vicious, not loud, yet twice as intimidating for the low tone. Charlie swallowed, more hurt than alarmed by his anger. Guilt gnawed at her because she knew he had a valid point. He'd obviously had everything under control, but for the first time in her life, she'd panicked. The realization was so new, so alien, she couldn't quite fathom it.

Of all the stupid things, she'd fallen in love with Harry Lonnigan.

"That was one of Carlyle's henchmen, you know. He'll tell him we were there. If you hadn't blundered,

I could have looked my fill with no one the wiser. But now, they know we know where they're at, and odds are they'll move. Tracking the idiots will be twice as difficult after this!"

She had no idea what to say. They'd been through a lot together already, and not once had Harry sounded so fed up, or so disgusted with her. Slowly, she sank into her seat and relatched her seat belt. She stared out the window, hoping to collect her thoughts enough to offer an excuse, a reply of some kind. But how could she tell him that she cared, that she was worried about him? Obviously the man was big enough, tough enough, to take care of himself without her questionable assistance, so she surely couldn't use that excuse. And mentioning love, or any type of emotion, was out of the question. Harry had been very clear on his feelings for her. He didn't even want her anymore and did his best to fight her off. She was such an uncouth yokel compared to his sophistication and background. She hadn't thought of it before, but now she had no choice.

The ride home was made in painful silence. Several times Charlie glanced at him, wincing in sympathy over his swollen, bruised eye. But the mulish set to his mouth, the hard glitter in his eyes, kept her from commenting on it.

After Harry had turned the car off in the parking garage he drew a deep breath and faced her. "Where's your truck?"

She shrugged, doing her best to look cavalier. "I parked on the street."

"Charlie..."

That sympathetic tone of his made her spine stiffen. She didn't want his pity, especially when he refused to share anything else.

Various emotions seemed to bombard her, wearing her down, but she was made of pretty stern stuff, not one to wilt when things went sour. So she wanted him? It was in her nature to fight for what she wanted, but this situation was different, wanting a man. She knew he desired her, and that had strengthened her resolve, but it was also obvious he didn't want to desire her, and she could understand his reasonings very easily.

Pride forced her to give in graciously, to salvage what she could of her self-respect. She worked up an icy smile, then opened her car door before looking at him. "I've decided to let you off the hook."

The swelling black eye seemed obscene on his handsome face. He didn't move, just sat there staring at her. "What the hell are you talking about?"

She lifted one shoulder. "I won't pester you anymore. I've decided to quit playing spy and get back to my own business. The bar doesn't run itself and I've neglected it these last few days. If you want to send me a bill for what I owe you—"

His good eye narrowed, giving her pause.

"—for the info on my father, I mean. I'll get the money to you right away."

"I haven't finished telling you what I know of your father."

Though she wasn't a coward, had never been a coward, she wanted to leap out of the car and run away. She didn't want to continue sitting there, chatting like everything was fine when she'd just had the most astounding realization of her life. There were very few people she'd ever loved, and other than Jill, they'd all been mistakes. She hated to think of Harry that way.

"That's all right. You said he hadn't completely abandoned us, so I'm assuming he'll pay what he owes. That's all I really need to know. I can have a lawyer contact him. Or maybe I'll just send him a letter..."

Harry reached for her and she slid quickly out of the car, dodging him. If he touched her, she'd want to touch him back, and she was determined not to make a bigger fool of herself. "Thanks for the help, Harry. I can handle it from here."

He, too, left the car and slowly stood to face her. The slamming of his door echoed around the empty garage. She closed hers more carefully. When Harry started around the car toward her, she began backstepping to the entrance. She tried an airy wave. "It's been...fun."

His growl reminded her of a rabid animal. He kept coming, his narrowed eyes looking more lethal than ever with the dark bruise and the swelling. He was large and imposing and somehow all his sophistication seemed to have melted away under his basic masculinity. "You're coming inside with me."

Her spine stiffened. "No thanks. I need to get going."

"I'm not asking, Charlie. I'm giving an explicit mandate. We have things to talk about, and I'm fed up with your unaccountable stubbornness and scurrility."

"I don't even know what that word means, Harry." He looked like he might lunge at her any minute, so she kept backing up. Unfortunately she didn't look behind her, and she fetched up against a concrete wall, clunking her head. "Ow."

While she rubbed her head, he closed in on her, using his long muscled arms to cage her in, stepping so close she could feel his warmth and breathe in his hot scent. He stared at her face, at her eyes and her mouth. She felt the gentle touch of his breath, and the blast of his temper, in sharp contrast.

"It means," he said succinctly, "that cutting wit of yours which you dispense with no thought to consequences and without evident remorse."

She forgot she wanted away from him, or even that her head hurt. Her own temper snapped and she leaned closer to taunt, "Oh, poor baby. Have I said something to hurt your feelings?"

His jaw worked. They were so close her nose bumped his chin. Then he took her arm in an unbreakable grip, stepped back, and headed for the town house. She got dragged in his wake. "No, but I do believe you prodded me into hurting yours. And for that, I'm sorry."

"What nonsense! I don't need an apology from you. Really... *Harry*, let me go!"

"No."

He tugged and pulled and coerced her along until they reached his door. Losing a fight really went against the grain, so she doubled her efforts. She didn't want to hurt him, so she was at a distinct disadvantage. She tried going limp, hoping her weight would throw him off-guard, but he managed to control her by the expedient method of wrapping one arm around her and lifting her off her feet. Mortified, Charlie went perfectly still.

He unlocked the door with his free hand and stepped inside to the sounds of excited barking. With a laugh, Harry released her to relock the door, and Charlie, seeing red, gave up on trying to get away from him. Instead, she launched her own attack. She took Harry off-guard and he stumbled and with the dogs flying around their feet and Ted screeching out a raucous complaint, they went down on the floor, hard.

Unfortunately, Charlie was on the bottom.

HARRY DODGED A tight fist aimed for his bruised eye. He'd expected no less of Charlie, especially since he was well aware of her more bloodthirsty tendencies. But for a moment there, she'd seemed too withdrawn, almost sad, and the thought that he might have hurt her feelings with his temper had been a squeezing pain in his heart. When he'd seen that thug leaning on the Jag, talking to her... He never wanted to feel that possessive, that protective or enraged again.

She swung at him again, demanding his immediate attention. Laughing, he captured her hands and pinned them over her head. The dogs were going crazy, taking the struggle as a free-for-all game. Sooner jumped close enough to stick a wet snout in Harry's ear, then dodged away again, howling maniacally. Charlie got a gleeful lap across the temple from Grace, and she struggled even more, cursing Harry and trying to discourage the dogs.

Her wriggling body had a very basic effect on him. He looked down at her, seeing the way her short, glossy black hair tumbled around her head, the way her cheeks flushed with her efforts. She lurched up against him, her head thrown back, her teeth catching her bottom lip, and he nearly groaned. Damn, she looked like a woman in the throes of a climax.

Her legs were caught under his and she tried to kick one free. Harry used his knee to spread her thighs, then settled between them. This time when she lunged upward, there was no way she could mistake his state of arousal. He had a throbbing erection and she froze.

The dogs moved in, taking advantage of the inactivity, whining and barking and nudging the humans. Harry barely noticed. Charlie had opened her eyes and locked her gaze on his, and the emotional connection was so strong, so powerful compared to anything he'd ever felt, he couldn't move. It was like he was inside her already.

She gasped for breath and he raised himself slightly, not enough to let her get away, but enough so she could breathe. She immediately lifted herself to press against him again. She could drive him crazy, he thought, even as he settled his hips against hers, giving in to her silent demand. His pulse raced, his muscles drawing tight. It felt so right to be with her like this.

Her knees bent, and she slowly moved her pelvis against his in an unpracticed, voluptuous sway. Mesmerized, he watched her face, saw the trembling in her lips as she drew in a shaky breath, saw her beautiful blue eyes darken, saw her skin heat.

Sooner howled again and without looking away, Harry commanded, "Go lie down." The dogs complained, but they finally obeyed.

Charlie tried to pull her hands free, but he held tight. "No you don't. I like you like this," he whispered. "You need just a little controlling, someone to keep you in line."

Though her eyes were heavy lidded and filled with sensual need, she lifted her chin. "You have to let me up sometime."

As far as threats went, it held no weight. Harry leaned down and nuzzled the soft skin beneath that raised chin. "Who says?"

Her eyes drifted shut and she hooked her feet behind his thighs. "You feel so good, Harry. Will you make love to me now?"

Everything righted itself in that instant and his brain cleared. With a vicious curse he released her and sat up. She didn't. She remained sprawled on the floor beside him, offering the most delectable temptation man could imagine. He tried not to look at her, but he couldn't help himself.

"Damn, I'm sorry."

"I'm not," she whispered.

He ran a hand through his hair. "How do you keep doing this to me?"

"I didn't do anything except try to let you off the hook. You're the one who dragged me in here."

After a calming breath, he forced himself to say, "I don't want off the hook. And I'm sorry I yelled at you."

"All things considered, I'd kinda forgotten all about that."

He looked at her, lying there so sweet and submissive—surely a first for Charlie—and his muscles cramped in rebellion of what he knew he had to do. "Honey, this is all wrong. I brought you up here to talk about your father, not to...ravish you on the damn floor."

"I rather liked being ravished on the floor."

He couldn't help but laugh, she was so persistent and candid and honest. There wasn't a single ounce of guile in her expression, and the fact that she was as free, as unreservedly sexual as himself, made him crazy. She hadn't minded their rough play in the least, and wasn't offended at being debauched on a floor. She would be his sexual equal, and knowing it made his arousal even more keen.

But she was Dalton's daughter, and Dalton would be appalled to know just how low Harry had sunk.

He stood, caught her arms, and pulled her to her feet. She stared up at him and he cupped her face. "Tell me you'll at least give your father a chance, okay?"

To his surprise, she seemed to be considering it. "Why is it so important to you, Harry?"

With complete and utter honesty, he said, "Because I think he's a good man and he loves you. I think he deserves a chance to tell his side of the story. And because I was never able to connect with my own father. It's something that bothers me still, something that every so often vexes me because now the man is gone and more often than not I don't even mourn him. I don't want you to ever suffer that, to wonder if only you'd softened a bit you could have had a wonderful relationship. For Jill's sake, for all it will mean to her, why don't you at least try?"

Harry held his breath, praying she'd relent. With any luck at all, Dalton would be getting out of the hospital today. Harry didn't want him under unnecessary stress, and he knew Dalton would stew endlessly about the situation until he was reunited with his daughters. If Charlie would agree, it could be taken care of within a week. That would give her time to prepare and give Dalton time to rebuild his strength.

Also, Harry's control was almost at an end. For his own sanity, he had to tie up loose ends so he could distance himself from her before he made a mistake he'd live to regret. Dalton deserved his loyalty, and Charlie deserved a man who would love her forever.

Unfortunately, the thought of her with another man made his system revolt, so he quickly shoved that thought aside.

Harry had no idea which part of his discourse convinced her, but after several moments of deep thought, she nodded. "All right." She hesitated, then stepped close and embraced him. "Will you...go with me?"

Harry wrapped his arms around her and held her tight, too tight, judging by her laughing, mumbled complaint. He didn't understand the near desperate urge to hold her, but he knew her embrace hadn't been designed to seduce him this time. Rather, it was the need for emotional comfort, and it touched him to his very soul. She willingly showed him her vulnerable side, something she normally kept well hidden, and he'd never felt so gifted in his entire life.

Though he knew it would be incredibly awkward, he kissed her temple and nodded. "Of course I'll be there."

She leaned back with a relieved smile. "When?"

He couldn't make her any promises until he found out how Dalton had fared. He'd called the hospital when he first got up, and the nurse had told him all seemed well. Dalton had been in high spirits, anxious to know what Harry had planned—a tale Harry related with precise discretion, leaving out any reference that might upset Dalton. He hadn't spoken to him again since the doctor's visit, and now he was anxious to do so. He led Charlie to the door, though he was equally reluctant to let her go.

With a last kiss on her forehead, which was a habit he desperately needed to break, he said, "Try not to worry, honey. I'll arrange everything as soon as I can, and then I'll let you know."

She smiled up at him, her eyes big and soft and filled with gratitude. "Thanks, Harry. I know it's stupid, and if you ever tell anyone I'll deny it, but it's kind of a relief that I don't have to do this alone. I owe you."

As she left, his guilt doubled until it nearly consumed him. Damn it, what would she think when she found out he'd known Dalton all along? Would she understand? Or would she likely feel betrayed by the one person she'd started to trust? The worry gnawed at him, making him angry with regret, until the phone rang.

It was Dalton, and he was ready to come home.

9

THE SECOND Harry stepped through the barroom doorway, he could tell Charlie was nervous. He'd spent the past week with her, and her mannerisms and mood were very familiar to him now. He picked up on the small frown, the way she repeatedly swallowed. She was behind the thick, scarred wooden bar, a clipboard clutched tightly in her hand, taking some kind of inventory. Beside him, Dalton looked around in horrified disbelief.

"My God. She can't actually work here?"

Pulling his gaze from Charlie, Harry said, "She does, and she manages quite credibly. I don't think it's been easy for her, but she's the type of woman who once she sets her mind on something, it gets accomplished one way or another." Harry knew there was a wealth of pride in his tone, but he couldn't seem to help himself. He *was* proud, and he wanted Dalton to be, too.

The bar wasn't yet open. Charlie had insisted they meet there, partly, Harry assumed, because she felt it gave her an advantage to be on her own territory and in familiar surroundings. She wouldn't admit it, not even to herself, but she was very uncertain about meeting her father.

Her insecurity, and the need to hide it, endeared her

to Harry all the more. He smiled toward her, though Charlie was still unaware of them. They were early, but keeping Dalton away any longer had proved impossible.

Harry had convinced Dalton to wait a week, to give himself plenty of time to recover. He refused to let Harry tell Charlie about his heart attack, so there was no telling how Charlie would react during the meeting, but Harry thought it a safe bet she'd be antagonistic and stubborn. She had a lot of past grievances to get through before she'd be able to fully accept Dalton.

Harry found himself very ambiguous about the meeting. He worried for Dalton, though the doctor had said he was fine. Other than routine checkups and a warning to take life easier, Dalton was free to do as he pleased.

Harry also worried for Charlie. This wouldn't be easy for her, having the foundation of her resentment pulled out from under her. Today she would find out her mother had been a bitter, vindictive woman, and Harry would have done just about anything to shield her from that.

But he had another motive for putting the reunion off until today.

Over the past week he'd spent nearly every day with her, arguing, doing his best to protect her when she insisted on forcing her way into danger. Whenever he tried to accomplish something without her, she threatened to go off on her own. But despite her interference, he'd learned quite a bit about Carlyle, while keeping Charlie in the dark. She might suspect a few things, but thankfully, she had no solid evidence of his plans. If she had, she wouldn't have agreed to meet her father today.

Harry was counting on the meeting to keep her busy until everything was finally resolved.

Dalton was still looking around, his expression appalled. Harry had been in the bar many times, however, and the bar was empty with the lights turned up and no cigarette smoke to cloud the air. True, the lime green was almost blinding. But the place was tidy, and comforting in a lived in, relaxed sort of way. The wooden floor wasn't highly polished, but it was immaculately clean, and though some of the round, mismatched tables looked less than elegant, they were sturdy and in good repair. The walls were bare except for the occasional unframed poster, curling at the edges.

She'd obviously done the best she could with the bar, and Harry hoped Dalton would see that. Charlie had been given too much responsibility and too few breaks in her young life, and Harry was more than a little relieved to introduce her to her father, knowing Dalton would offer her new opportunities.

"Damn it, I wish Jill was going to be here. Charlotte's just being stubborn."

It was an unending refrain, and Harry sighed. They still hovered in the doorway, preferring to survey the bar and Charlie without notice. With a hand on Dalton's shoulder, Harry reminded him, "She doesn't yet know you, and she's fiercely protective of Jill. Until she's certain you won't disappoint or hurt her, I think you'll just have to be patient. In a way, that should reassure you, because you can tell Charlie's taken excellent care of her sister."

Dalton's hands fisted. "Damn Rose. None of this was necessary. If only the woman hadn't tried to punish me by running off."

"True, but go easy on what you say today," Harry advised. "Rose is the only parent Charlie knows, and I have a feeling her stubbornness would force her to be defensive even about that. And remember, I'm just a P.I. I don't want her to have to deal with my deception today, on top of everything else."

With that last reminder, Harry determined to get the whole thing going. He wanted to see Charlie and Dalton settled, so he could attend Carlyle's little surprise party.

He stepped forward and cleared his throat.

Charlie jerked her gaze up, then stilled. Harry could see the near panic in her beautiful eyes, and it smote him clear down to his masculine core. He wanted to hold her, but of course, he couldn't. "Hello, Charlie. I'm sorry we're early, but your father was a bit anxious."

Very slowly, her gaze shifted from Harry to her father. She looked like a small animal caught in the headlights of an oncoming car, but only for a moment. Harry saw the resolve stiffen her spine, saw her summon that indomitable courage. He felt emotion expand inside him, and though it scared him spitless, he smiled.

Charlie plunked down the clipboard, skirted the bar, and started toward them with a swanky, confident walk. Her clothes were even more disreputable today, her jeans well worn and a tad frayed at the hem, her boots scuffed. She wore a T-shirt with a suggestive beer logo on the front. It was at least two sizes too big, tucked into her snug jeans, and Harry thought she looked adorable.

Judging by the expression on Dalton's face, he didn't.

All nervousness had disappeared from Charlie's mien. She stood within a few feet of them, hands on her slim hips, feet spaced apart. She could have been facing Floyd and Ralph again for all her arrogant bravado.

"So." She glanced at each of them, then focused on Harry. "I had a delivery this morning I had to deal with. Usually I'm not even up till ten, given the hours I'm open, but the delivery guys always come early. I'd almost forgotten about them after the week we've had."

Harry didn't even want to think about that and cast a quick glance at Dalton to see if he'd caught the insinuation. Dalton had no idea Charlie had involved herself with the embezzlers, and he'd be twice as upset if he found out. But Dalton still stared at Charlie, and thankfully, looked unaware of the conversation.

Harry had tried refusing to let her accompany him as he continued checking into things, partly because he'd feared for her safety, and partly because he didn't trust his dubious control around her. It boggled the mind the way she could push his buttons, but damn if she didn't manage it every time she got near. She laughed and he wanted her. She stuck her stubborn chin in the air and he went hot with lust. And her eyes—when she looked at him with her sultry, bold expressions, it took all he had not to give in to the urge to have her.

Over the past week, he'd twice found her snooping on her own. The urge to put her over his knee had been overwhelming, and had dampened his carnal appetites. Yet when he'd offered that threat, she'd merely laughed, proving she knew he'd never hurt her. To his chagrin, *she* was the one who discovered Carlyle hadn't moved his operation at all. Evidently the man was so cocky he was totally without caution, disregarding Harry's interference as a threat.

After today, Carlyle would have to rethink that.

Harry looked at Dalton, who remained mute, and decided he'd have to get the ball rolling before Charlie disclosed things better left concealed. "Charlie, this is your father, Dalton Jones."

She tilted her head at Dalton, studying him closely. "You don't look as old as I had you pictured."

Dalton smiled nervously. "Did your mother show you any photographs of me?"

"Sure. But they were years ago. Eighteen years ago to be exact."

Dalton's eyes closed briefly and he nodded. "Eighteen years that I regret more than I can ever tell you."

His words and tone were so heartfelt, Charlie wavered. Harry could see her expression shift, the uncertainty come into her eyes. He took her arm and said gently, "Why don't we sit down? You two have a lot to talk about."

Once they were at a round table toward the middle of the floor, Charlie looked at Harry with a slight smile. "Your eye is healing—the bruises are only green now instead of black. But you still look wiped out. If you can keep from strangling on it, I'll go get some coffee from the back and we'll see if that can revive you."

He smiled, too, pleased to see the appearance of her wit. "I promise to only sip, to cut back on the chances of strangulation."

She glanced at Dalton and hesitated before asking, "Would you like some, too?"

He nodded. "Actually, Charlotte, I'd love some. Black, please."

Harry winced at the name, but quickly forestalled the storm he saw brewing on Charlie's face by saying, "Isn't that just how you take yours, Charlie? Black?"

Her smile turned sickly sweet. "Just." She walked away without another word.

When she was out of sight, Harry turned to frown at Dalton. It wasn't his place, but still he said, "She prefers to be called Charlie."

Dalton pulled out a chair and sat down, prompting Harry to do the same. With his back to the kitchen doorway Charlie had gone through, Dalton whispered, "It's a horrid nickname, probably her mother's doing, which is a good reason for me not to follow suit."

"God." Harry rubbed his face, unsure how to convince Dalton he should back off. Charlie definitely wasn't a woman you wanted to push, and especially not when she felt cornered emotionally.

Dalton stared around the bar with a grimace. "Don't you see? She deserves better than this, and it's my duty to see to it. She's wearing grubby clothes and working in a dump, when I want her to be free to be a young lady. I'll worry myself into an early grave if I have to think about her being here every night. I can help her now. She can sell this place and get a respectable diner or something instead. Or she could work for me at the jewelry store." His face brightened with the prospect. "You know I'd love to have her there."

"You're jumping the gun, don't you think?"

"Ha! She deserves a lot better than working in a place like this."

The sudden stillness in the air was palpable and Harry jerked around to see Charlie frozen behind them, a tray with coffee, mugs, cream and sugar in her hands. Her jaw was positively rigid, her face pale. There was such a wounded expression in her eyes, he knew he'd never forget it as long as he lived.

He and Dalton both stood. Dalton, fidgeting nervously, took the tray from her and put it on the table, then held out a chair. As she sat, Harry touched her arm, but she shook him off. Dalton poured coffee while she stared at him.

"You know, Jill looks a lot like you."

Her calm, controlled tone reassured Dalton. But it didn't fool Harry for a single second. She was up to something, and he knew it wouldn't be pleasant. He cleared his throat. "You all have the same blue eyes."

Dalton grinned. "I'm anxious to meet Jill. Though from what Harry has told me, she's lovely and doesn't look a thing like me."

Charlie shook her head. "You've got the same color hair, the same smile. And you both look the same when you feel guilty." She ignored Dalton's searching glance. "I look more like my mother."

"Yes, you do. And she was beautiful."

"Not toward the end she wasn't. She'd led a hard life, always drinking too much, smoking, never getting enough sleep. We found out she had emphysema and she had to go on oxygen. She hated it, because dragging the oxygen around made her feel old, but she was always tired, so she used it when she absolutely had to. One day she got pneumonia and just died."

Charlie recited the facts as if it had been a play, something unreal that had happened to someone else. Without even realizing his intent, Harry took her hand. She clutched at him, but her gaze never left Dalton.

"This *dump* paid for her funeral. It's also kept my sister clothed and fed for the last few years when I had no idea where you were." Charlie tilted her head, and her grin was without an ounce of humor. "And of course, it's given me the opportunity to be free."

Dalton, already looking stricken by what she'd said, asked cautiously, "Free?"

Charlie shrugged. "I'm my mother's daughter. Did you think she hadn't told me? I knew she'd cheated on you and I heard all her excuses for why you should have forgiven her. She blamed you completely, you know, because she said you weren't around often enough. Even if she hadn't told me, her character was pretty plain to see for anyone with eyes, much less a daughter who lived with her. So what makes you think I'm any different?"

Dalton blustered. "Well, I never thought... I mean, that wasn't the indication I was..."

Charlie pulled Harry's arm over and hugged it to her breasts. Harry, taken off-guard, gawked at her.

She laughed. "Harry didn't tell you that? Well, of course he didn't. Harry is a gentleman, and gentlemen never kiss and tell."

She leaned over and lightly kissed Harry on the jaw, and he stiffened. When he got her alone, he planned to throttle her. "Charlie—"

"I appreciate your efforts on my behalf, Harry. But whether Dalton likes it or not, the bar suits me. I'd go nuts in a nine-to-five atmosphere with rules and restrictions and you know it. Besides, the men here are always so complimentary—when they're not too tanked to get the compliments out."

Harry locked his jaw and struggled to think of a way to get her off-track. He understood her, knew exactly what she was doing, but he didn't like being used.

"Now Harry, he's such a smooth talker, he never runs out of compliments." At Dalton's unblinking stare, she added, "You didn't think he only *worked* for me, did you? No, Harry and I have gotten real close."

Harry cursed when Dalton looked at him, brows raised in question.

At a momentary loss, Dalton swallowed hard. Finally he shook his head. "I understand how difficult your life must have been, Charlotte, believe me. But I'm here now and—"

"And I've been doing as I please too long to start restricting myself at this late date." Her tone was hard, uncompromising. "If you hoped to step in and play father by correcting all my faults, forget it. I happen to revel in my faults."

Dalton directed a commanding look at Harry, then slowly stood. "I... Could you excuse me a moment?"

Charlie nodded, watching him with narrowed eyes. "Sure thing. Boy's room is in the back, down the hallway and to your left."

Harry, having correctly interpreted that look, started to follow, but Charlie didn't let him go.

He turned on her, as furious with the situation as he was with her absurd theatrics. "What the hell are you doing, making him think you're...we're..."

"Lovers?" She made a face and sipped her coffee. "Why not? He obviously thinks I'm lacking and has some harebrained idea of reforming me. This way, he'll know right off it's a lost cause and not start meddling in my life."

Harry sank back into his seat. Dalton could wait for the moment. He turned Charlie's hand so he could lace their fingers together. "He thinks no such thing. He's very proud of you, he just wants to help."

"Ha!"

Harry grimaced. He was getting damn sick and tired of that expression.

"I heard what he said, Harry. He wants to help me get my life straightened out, but it's the truth, I enjoy my life. Other than wishing I could give more to Jill, I wouldn't change a thing."

Harry knew that wasn't merely pride talking. The bar was home to her, and she wouldn't give it up easily. He sighed. "All right, so tell him that, but don't

start pretending there's something going on between
us—"

"Isn't there? Well, okay, not as much as I suggested,
but I was on your floor the other night, Harry, and I
enjoyed what you did to me. I'd like us to do it again."

"Damn it, Charlie...."

"You're working for me, right? So consider this a
side assignment—with bonus pay."

Harry narrowed his eyes. "You're pushing me."

She leaned toward him with a wicked grin. "I like
pushing you." Then the grin was gone, replaced by a
stubborn set to her mouth. "But this is important. And
since you *are* working for me, I figured you wouldn't
mind helping me dupe him just a little bit. I know it
pushes the boundaries of reality to think of us actually
involved in anything more than a quick fling, but Dalton can't know that. So what's the big deal?"

Harry groaned.

"If he really does care, which I have serious doubts
about, it won't matter to him what I do or who I am.
And if it does matter, well, then, he can give me the
money for Jill's education and get lost for another
eighteen years. The money is all I really care about
anyway."

Harry stared at her, knowing she lied. He could see
it in her eyes, how much her father's apparent disapproval had hurt her, and he decided to give Dalton a
piece of his mind.

"I'm going to check on him. Stay put, okay?"

"Did you think I'd run off and hide? Not likely."

Harry found Dalton standing in the tiny gray bathroom. The walls were painted brick and cement, the

ceiling light a bare bulb. Dalton looked at Harry with bleak eyes. "She can't really like this place."

Harry crossed his arms over his chest and leaned against the door. "You know, Dalton, I've gotten to know Charlie—and *yes*, she is Charlie whether you like it or not!"

Dalton subsided, biting back his complaint.

"I've gotten to know her beyond what she presents to most of the world."

Dalton quirked a brow. "So she said."

Harry waved that off. "That's just her way of getting even for your censure. She wanted to hurt you, the way you hurt her."

"But I didn't mean to hurt her! I just wanted her to know she has choices now."

"I know that, but she doesn't. She's a wonderful, caring, independent woman who prides herself on those qualities. I have the feeling she's never asked anyone for anything, and coming to you now for money really rubs her the wrong way."

"It shouldn't. I'd gladly give her anything I have."

"But don't you see? She's always been able to get by on her own through gumption and strength of will. She turned this run-down dive into a favored local saloon, and she's supported her sister and ailing mother by doing so. I've watched her working here. From the regulars to the occasional drop-in, Charlie deals with them all in her own special way, protecting herself, but not really offending, being friendly, but never letting any man get too close." *Except for himself.* He shoved that thought aside and continued. "She's rightfully proud of this place and what she's accomplished. When you insult it, you insult her."

Dalton rubbed his face. "It's just so—"

"Not what you'd expected? What you'd want for her? I never thought to say it, but you remind me of my own father, Dalton."

That got his attention, his head snapping up and he frowned.

"She has to lead her own life, not the life you'd choose for her. All you can do now is be there for her. She's twenty-seven years old, a grown woman, and frankly I don't think she needs to change."

Dalton drew back, both brows shooting high. "You sound like you care about her."

Through his teeth, Harry said, "I like her as a friend."

"Hmm."

Harry decided it was time to change the subject. "Dalton, she has this crazy idea of making you think we're lovers. I have to tell her the truth."

"No! I think this might be the perfect opportunity. I screwed up, I admit it, but maybe I can fix things." He began pacing back and forth in front of the sink. "I never meant for her to hear me, it's just that I'm anxious to help. But now I can prove to her that I do care. As long as she's only acting with you, I'll know she's safe. I'll be able to show her that I accept her, that I..." He swallowed hard, his eyes misty. "That I love her no matter what."

Harry's insides cramped. "That's an asinine plan."

"No, don't you see? She's doing this to shock me because she thinks I'll walk away repulsed. But now I can show her I'll never leave her again, no matter what."

Harry muttered a crude curse that had Dalton blinking in surprise.

"All right. But I'm telling you, I don't like it. You'd better prove yourself to her and fast because I can't take too much more."

Harry stomped out of the bathroom without explaining what it was he couldn't take, and almost ran over Charlie, who'd come to see why it was taking them so long. He caught her to keep her from falling, and she landed against his chest with a thud. She saw Dalton behind Harry, and that was all the encouragement she needed. She threw her arms around his neck, plastered her body up against his, and kissed him so thoroughly he thought he was having his own heart attack.

"I just got off the phone," she whispered against his mouth. "I found someone to cover for me so I could have the night off. I guess we've got a date after all."

10

CHARLIE ALMOST laughed at the look on Harry's face. He went from heated response, to shock, to chagrin. Luckily her father was still behind him and didn't see that variety of reactions. She kissed him again for good measure, and as he removed her arms with a chastising frown and started around her, she patted his butt.

Harry jumped, looking like a man who'd just been stung, then took her hand and literally dragged her to the table. Dalton came along, smiling like a damn Cheshire cat, though what he had to grin about, Charlie had no idea.

When they reached the table, Harry pulled a chair out for her. She laughed, pushed him into his seat and dropped onto his lap. She was prepared to put on a real show, not only to prove to her father she was beyond redemption, but because this gave her the perfect opportunity to be close to Harry. Very soon now, their time would be over. He'd brought her father to her, and he planned to wrap things up that week with Floyd and Ralph. He wouldn't share his plans in that regard, but she'd come to know Harry very well and knew he was up to something. Just the fact that he'd been hanging out in the Lucky Goose all week told her he wanted to keep an eye on her, to make sure she didn't blunder into whatever plans he had in mind.

It didn't bother her. She was so at ease with Harry, she could enjoy his company while being herself.

To her surprise, Harry didn't try to push her away. He sighed, then looped his arms around her waist. In her ear, he whispered, "There's always retribution to be paid, Charlie. Don't forget that."

She ignored this threat, just as she ignored all his others. Harry wouldn't hurt her and she knew it. She turned to Dalton, to judge his reaction to the scene, and saw him staring toward the doorway. With an inkling of dread, she whipped about and there stood Jillian. She had a shopping bag clutched in her hands and a frozen expression on her face.

"Oh hell." Charlie started to scramble off Harry's lap, but he tightened his hold.

"Ah, ah. Don't turn cowardly on me now."

"Harry, I don't want Jill—"

"To meet her father?" He gave her a gentle hug. "Honey, relax. It'll be okay."

"Not with me on your lap! What will she think?"

"That you're up to mischief again, no doubt."

Dalton came to his feet like a sleepwalker. "Jillian?"

Jillian's smile trembled the tiniest bit, and then she walked forward cautiously. She glanced at Charlie, and her eyes widened when she saw how her sister was seated. Charlie groaned. "It's not what you—"

Laughing, Harry interjected, "I'd stand, but you can see I have a vexatious burden in my lap."

Jill nodded politely. "Is there, ah, any reason why?"

With a smile that was pure wickedness, Harry said, "We're passionately involved, don't you know."

Charlie's elbow came back hard enough to make him grunt, then she smiled at Jill. "I was going to tell you later, after...well, I wanted to make sure everything would be okay..."

Jill glanced at Dalton, then back to her sister. "I understand. Would you like to introduce me now?"

"I suppose I don't really have a choice, do I? Jill, this is our father, Dalton Jones."

Jill caught her breath and dropped her bag. She blinked hard, trying to fend off tears. "I thought...I mean, you look exactly as I imagined, but I just wasn't sure..."

Dalton, his own eyes wet, reached out to her. "I never gave up hope of finding you."

Jill took his hands. "I have so many questions."

"Me, too."

They seemed to be in their own little world and Charlie, disgusted and a tad jealous, shook her head. Her sister was so much more accepting than she could ever be. She leaned back against Harry and whispered, "Don't start looking smug. If he does one thing to insult her or upset her, I'll toss him—and you—out."

Frowning, Harry appeared to consider that. "I don't think you can just toss a lover out. No, a lover gets to stick around through thick and thin."

"You're enjoying yourself, aren't you?"

"I'm beginning to."

Charlie looked at his totally shameful grin and had to smile herself. He did enjoy matching wits with her, that had been apparent from the first. She enjoyed it too, along with a great many other things.

She forgot about provoking Dalton and leaned forward to kiss him. Jill cleared her throat.

"Oh." Charlie straightened, flustered, while Harry looked sublimely unaffected.

"Don't mind us," he said, "she just can't keep her hands off me."

With a smothered laugh, Jill said, "I'm going to run upstairs and put my stuff away, then I'll be right back down."

Dalton stepped forward. "You live upstairs, is that correct?"

"Yes. Would you like me to show you around?"

Charlie stiffened, ready to refuse despite Harry's gentle stroking on her back, when Jill added, a touch of warning in her tone, "Charlie won't mind. She never lets men upstairs—well, except for Harry, but he's different."

"So I understand."

Jill laughed. "Charlie is rigidly uncompromising about how she handles having our home above the bar. She's never wanted any of the men here to get the wrong idea. She won't admit it, but she's something of a mother hen most of the time."

Dalton glanced at Charlie with a smile. "I realize that. And it soothes me to know what a wonderful job she's done handling everything."

Charlie's mouth fell open in surprise at the praise, and Harry started to laugh, tempting Charlie's elbow again. She gave in to temptation, and at the same time prompted her sister with, "I thought you were going to put your things away."

Jill rolled one shoulder. "I don't know why you're so shy about being a good sister. It's not like it's a bad thing."

Dalton took Jill's arm to start them on their way. "Maybe you can tell me more about...Charlie, during our tour?"

"I'd love to!"

As they disappeared through the doorway, Charlie dropped back against Harry with a groan. "Jill and her big mouth."

Harry smiled against her temple. "If I laugh, will you poke me with that sharp elbow of yours again?"

"Absolutely."

"Then I'll content myself with telling you how childish you're acting." She started to pull away, but he locked his arms around her, just below her breasts, and held her secure. "Allow your lover just a little leeway, please. It's my right as such to point these things out."

"Okay, so pretending we're involved was a bad idea on my part. You can quit punishing me for it."

"Is that what I was doing?"

"Yes. You've made your point. I've acted like a total idiot."

"I never said any such thing and I'll thank you not to put words in my mouth."

She twisted to face him, bracing her hands on his shoulders. "All right, so what would you say?"

He smoothed her hair away from her face and his expression grew serious, his golden brown eyes intent. "That you're fighting yourself more than anyone else. Dalton's reaction wasn't one of disapproval, but guilt. He doesn't know you well enough yet to know you wouldn't be taken advantage of. He doesn't know how strong and capable you are."

"But you do?"

His hand cupped her neck, caressing. "You're the strongest person I've ever met."

"Too strong?"

His brows lifted in admission. "Sometimes. You plow your way through life assuming sheer determination will get you what you want."

She wondered if he was talking about himself. True, she'd been coming on strong, but that was the only way she knew. Sheer determination *had* gotten her everything she wanted—with the exception of a responsible mother or an available father.

She looked down at his chest and toyed with a button on his shirt. "Today...well, this was just for show."

"I wasn't talking about us, Charlie. I was talking about this unreasonable assumption you have that you can handle men like Carlyle, or even Floyd and Ralph."

"Oh." She waved that away. "I'm not worried about them, even though you're keeping secrets from me." She slanted him a look. "I know something's going on, and I'll figure it out sooner or later. Now, don't look like that, Harry. You know I will! I'm not dumb, and despite all your warnings, they don't scare me."

His sigh was exaggerated. "I know, and that's what

worries me. I have enough appreciation for their malevolent capacities for both of us."

Charlie grinned. "I love it when you talk like that. *Malevolent capacities*. It sounds dirty."

He shook her slightly, but she could see the amusement in his eyes. "I'm serious here, Charlie."

"Yeah, well, I'm seriously starting to wonder what's taking them so long. Our apartment is pretty small. You could walk the whole thing in under two minutes."

"You're incorrigible."

"Tell my father that." Harry grew so solemn, she sighed. "All right, I'm sorry."

He grabbed his head and weaved in the chair, almost toppling Charlie. "I must be delirious. Surely you didn't just apologize? Not Charlie Jones, the toughest—"

"My elbow hasn't gotten any softer you know." She stifled a chuckle as she made the threat, drawing her arm back in warning.

Harry grabbed her close and kissed her mouth, laughing against her lips. It was a ticklish kiss—at least at first. Then his mouth softened, slowed with awareness. She was on his lap, feeling his heat, his strength. At first the closeness was a game, but now it struck her how cozy it could be.

She'd never sat in a man's lap before meeting Harry.

They both remained motionless for a long moment, and Charlie could hear the thundering of her heartbeat in her ears. Her lips parted, and with a groan, Harry tilted her back over his arm. His mouth was suddenly hot, hungry, his tongue stroking past her lips, tasting—

"Maybe we should leave the lovebirds alone."

Harry jerked back so fast he made Charlie lose her balance. She almost slid off his lap. He managed to catch her arms, saving her the disgrace of falling on her behind. To her disgust, she could feel her face heating.

"Ah, Jill, we were just..."

"I'm young, sis, not stupid." Jill shook her head at Harry, then continued. "Father and I have decided to go to dinner. He said you two had a date, so we'll just use the time to get better acquainted."

Charlie felt her temper start to boil, but then Dalton stepped closer and said, "That's if it's okay with you. Harry drove here, but we can catch a cab. I thought after dinner, I could show Jill the jewelry store I own on the other side of town. I'd love for you to see it as well, but of course, I don't want to interfere with your personal time."

Momentarily stuck in her own deception, Charlie said, "Uhhh...."

Harry had no such problem. "That's fine. I'm sure we'll manage without you."

Charlie stood and stared hard at Dalton in warning. "Where are you going to dinner?"

He didn't look the least put off by her tone, or her question. "I thought we'd go to Maria's. It's a nice little Italian restaurant not too far from my store."

It was a restaurant she'd never been to, a very ritzy, expensive place well above her budget. She glanced at her sister and saw that Jill had changed into a dress and looked very excited by the prospect of dining there. Charlie didn't want to let her go. Old protective instincts clamored inside her, reminding her of all the years she'd spent looking out for her sister's well-being. But Jill was eighteen now, a young woman, and it was time to give her some freedom.

It went against her instincts, but Charlie nodded. "All right."

Jill stepped forward and gave Charlie a tight hug. "Thank you."

She waved her off. "Don't thank me. I'm not the one taking you."

"But we both know I wouldn't go if you asked me not to."

Uncomfortable with Dalton and Harry listening in, Charlie made a face. "Yeah, well, I'm assuming Dalton will take good care of you."

Dalton's mouth twitched at the malice in her tone. "Absolutely." Then he, too, stepped forward for a hug, taking Charlie by surprise. In a low voice meant only for her ears, he said, "I can't tell you how pleased I am to finally meet you. Pleased, and so damn proud."

Charlie was still mute after they'd walked out the door. Harry, with a twisted grin, waved a hand in front of her face.

"Are you all right or did Dalton put a trance on you?"

She shook her head as if to clear it, then looked at Harry, but she didn't really see him. A jumbled mix of emotions made her shaky inside. *Her father was proud?* She swallowed hard and tried to digest that information, but every stubborn, fighting instinct she had rebelled against it. Accepting any accolades from him would make her weak, would detract from the foundation she'd built over the past months and alter her goals completely. It was too much to take in all at once, and so she did what came naturally instead.

With a determined look that made Harry draw back, she walked around him and started out of the bar.

He hustled after her. "Where are you off to, brat?"

"I'm going to follow them."

"*What?*"

"He can visit with my sister all he likes, as long as I'm close enough to take care of her if anything goes wrong." Using her key, she unlocked the bottom door and rushed through it. Harry caught it in time and went up the steps with her. "I'm going to change, then I'm leaving. If you want to come along, fine, but I don't need you there."

He tried to catch her arm, but she shook him off to unlock the door at the top of the stairs.

"Charlie, this is insane."

"Think what you like. I'm still going to do it." She went down the hall to her bedroom, aware of Harry right behind her, and of his shock to her decorating scheme. He'd been upstairs many times, but never in her bedroom.

He stood there with his mouth open, his face blank. "Good God. You have ruffles."

Belligerent, she said, "Yeah, so? It's my room and I can decorate it any way I want." She pulled out a clean pair of newer jeans and a white button-down oxford-cloth shirt. It was the closest thing she had to "dressier."

Harry touched the fluffy white quilt on her bed. "I like it, so don't sound so defensive. It's just that I pictured you with..."

"Barbed wire? A bare mattress?" She snorted. "The quilt is warm and the bed skirt hides all the stuff I stick under my bed."

Harry bent and looked. "There's nothing under your bed."

"Go to hell, Harry."

He laughed, but when she pulled off her T-shirt to change, his humor died a quick death. Sounding strangled, he asked, "What are you doing?"

"Changing. I can't very well go unnoticed if I wear what they've already seen."

"Charlie." With his gaze glued to her upper body, bare except for her bra, he clasped her shoulders. "Don't do this to yourself."

She tried to shrug him off, but his large hands held firm. "I have to hurry."

"You're not going anywhere, sweetheart."

Turmoil exploded inside her, making her hands shake and her stomach pitch. In a voice that was less than steady, she growled, "Don't start with me now, Harry. I *have* to go."

"Shh." Despite her resistance he pulled her close and his big hot hands smoothed up and down her naked spine. "I know, babe, I really do. This is so damn hard. But you need to indulge in a little trust."

"Trust a man I barely know?"

He kissed her ear, still making those "shushing"

sounds. "You know me, and I've told you the man is safe. And you should certainly trust your sister. What responsibilities did you have at eighteen?"

The trembling became worse and she leaned into Harry, for the moment letting herself relax, letting his heat seep into her. "None that I want Jill to have."

"You've done an incredible job with her, Charlie. She's an intelligent young lady and an excellent judge of character. She has enough sense to call you if anything should go wrong."

She bit her lip, trying to sort out her thoughts. "Why should I trust you when you don't trust me?"

His hands stilled.

"Something's going on with Carlyle. I can feel it."

A look of alarm passed over his features and his frown turned fierce. "That has nothing to do with you."

Flabbergasted, she leaned back to look at him. "And my personal life has nothing to do with *you*, but I noticed that hasn't slowed you down any!"

Her new posture pushed her pelvis closer to his, while baring her upper body. His gaze again lowered to her breasts, and he remained silent.

Tension radiated off him and she shifted. "What? No answer to that?"

His hand coasted down her spine to her backside, cuddling and stroking. In a near rasp, he said, "We're standing in a bedroom, you're taunting me with these luscious little breasts of yours, and I'm so aroused I can barely think. Did you really expect me to indulge in conversation?"

Her own arousal hit like a tidal wave, stealing her

breath and filling her with undulating heat. All her confusion, all her nervousness, magically transformed into sexual awareness. She could barely get a whisper past her constricted throat. "Harry?"

Shaking his head with a denial she didn't understand, he closed his eyes. "I can't do this anymore."

The heat of his hard chest beckoned her, and she braced her palms flat there. "Do what?"

Startling her with his suddenness, he lifted her, walked the two steps to the bed, then dropped with her to the mattress. He caught her hands and lifted them over her head, then groaned as her breasts pressed to his chest.

The weight of his body both appeased and intensified the ache, making her squirm. "I love how you feel, Harry. So hard and hot and strong."

The low gasping of his breath tickled her ear. "I'm glad you think so, because I'm in no hurry to move."

"I don't want you to move. Let my hands go."

"No."

"What do you mean 'no'?" When he didn't answer, she tried to pull away.

"Not this time, honey. This time we finish it. *My way.*"

Charlie felt both excited and slightly alarmed by his uncompromising tone, uncertain how she should react. Then she realized she really had no choice. Harry wasn't letting go, and that meant she'd have to accept whatever he had planned.

Her eyes narrowed sensually. She'd wallow in every second of his dominance.

RAISING HIMSELF slightly, Harry smiled and transferred both her hands into one of his own, then cupped her jaw. "You're just filled with demands, aren't you?"

"I wasn't..."

"Hmm. Yes, you were. It's part and parcel of who you are. But I like it. Most of the time. Right now, I like you soft and submissive beneath me." He kissed her gently, pulling back when she tried to deepen the kiss. "Do you like it too, honey?"

"Yes."

That soft whisper shook his resolve. Harry closed his mouth over hers, felt her lips part and immediately stroked his tongue inside. Her slender thighs tightened restlessly, her body shifting in subtle, erotic moves. His free hand slid down her side, then to her soft breast. Damn she felt good. Her nipple was already puckered, pressing against her thin cotton bra, and with a low curse, he caught the cup with his fingertips and pulled it down until her firm breast came free.

Harry tore his mouth away from hers to look at her. He leaned back and to the side, keeping her hands firmly clasped, watching in heated appreciation as she strained toward him.

Her breast was so white, the nipple a soft pale pink, and he wanted her. He leaned down with no forewarning and drew her into his mouth.

She gave a stifled scream.

"Hush. Someone downstairs might hear you."

"Harry...it's too much."

"Nonsense," he said, taunting her with his assurance. "You'll like this. Just be still."

She didn't even try. As he licked and gently sucked, she struggled against him, moaning, twisting. She kept trying to pull her hands free, but he didn't think she was even aware of it. She didn't want to be free, it was just in Charlie's nature to fight any type of restriction. He felt provoked by her reactions, and grew all the more determined to control things.

From the day he'd met her, she'd made him crazy with her take charge ways, even while his admiration for her courage grew. Little by little she'd seduced him, not just sexually, but emotionally as well. He wanted her, and he was tired of denying himself. Unlike his ex-wife, who tried to manipulate with tears, Charlie fought fair, with upfront demands and honest compromises. He enjoyed his battles with her, rather than feeling guilty over them. She excited him on every level, and he couldn't resist any longer.

Later, he'd work through the problems. But now, in this precise moment, all he cared about was making her his own.

He loved the taste of her, her hot reactions, and he wanted more. Coming up to his knees, straddling her hips so she couldn't scoot away, he tugged the bra completely off. Charlie froze for an instant as the heat of embarrassment colored her face and throat. "You're looking at me."

"Yes." With one finger he touched her exposed nipples. "You're wet from my mouth, tight and sweet."

Her eyes closed again and she made soft sounds of desire. Her breasts were plump, offered up by the way she kept straining toward him. The mere sight of her aroused him as much as an hour of foreplay. "You're right, sweetheart. These are very special."

"You're embarrassing me, Harry."

His mouth tipped in a small smile. She didn't sound embarrassed. She sounded excited. Her breasts shimmered with each breath, her diaphragm expanding. Her abdomen was silky smooth, narrow. The waistband of her jeans curled out away from her skin and he deftly flicked the snap free. He could hear her rasping, anxious breaths as he slowly tugged down the zipper. Her belly was taut, her hips staining upward. He dipped one fingertip in her navel, then followed the line of her zipper downward, gradually parting the material until he came to the elastic waistband of her bikini panties. Because he'd already seen her bra, he wasn't surprised that these were also white cotton.

"You have very conservative taste in underclothes," he murmured.

His finger continued to tickle up and down just inside her zipper and her voice shook when she replied. "No one sees them but me."

Her words filled him with satisfaction, and the possessive urges no longer alarmed him. "I think this one is jealous," he said of the breast he hadn't yet tasted.

"Harry..."

Her tone was a whimper in anticipation of what she knew would come. He wanted her to understand that she couldn't always control him, that some things were better left in his hands, especially the sensual things.

With that in mind, he bent and carefully kissed her

breast, avoiding the erect, puckered nipple and ignoring her soft cries. Relentlessly he teased, always staying just out of reach no matter how she turned or tried to coax him to take her into his mouth. She cursed him softly, then moaned, her thick lashes drifting down over her eyes, her body going utterly lax, with no fight left at all.

Harry tried to stifle the overwhelming feeling of triumph, but knowing he'd won with this one particular woman—and that she'd enjoyed letting him win— filled him with primitive instincts. He loosened his hold and whispered close to her ear, "Don't move, sweetheart."

"Harry...*please*."

His heart tripped. He'd never thought to hear that word from her mouth. She'd not only given over to him, she trusted him enough to show her full need. Releasing her hands and sitting up, Harry pulled off her boots and socks, then hooked his fingers in the waistband of her jeans and tugged them down to her knees. She helped him by kicking them off the rest of the way.

Charlie watched him through dazed eyes. Her soft mouth was slightly open, her hands resting above her head, the palms up and vulnerable. He shook he wanted her so badly.

Coming down on his elbow beside her, he kissed her hungrily and she groaned in relief. Impatient, he stroked his hand down her belly and below, cupping his fingers over her mound, feeling the heat of her, the dampness of the cotton panties. He could hear the race of his blood in his ears, and the sexy little sounds Charlie made.

She was already so close, and he'd barely begun. He leaned away from her and saw her hands were now fisted tightly, her chest heaving, her pale thighs clenched. He pushed his hand inside her panties and with his middle finger pressed and stroked. "You're so wet, honey. Do you like that?"

"*Yes.*"

She didn't hesitate in answering, though her reply was an almost incoherent hiss. He'd always loved watching a woman climax, but seeing Charlie, her head pressed back, her neck muscles straining, her pretty breasts heaving—it was more than he'd ever expected. More than he likely deserved. Very slowly, he worked one finger inside her. Though she was silky wet and very excited, she clenched his finger tightly. He groaned, imagining how she'd feel squeezing his erection. His heart pounded.

"Ah, Harry, I..."

"Does that hurt?" he whispered. His free arm was beside her head and he smoothed her silky dark hair away from her face.

She shook her head, then said, "A little. But don't stop."

"No, I won't stop." It pained him to smile, he was so aroused, but he felt full to bursting with love and contentment. He kissed her cheek, her nose, then used his thumb to find her small clitoris. He touched it lightly and she jerked, her reaction very telling.

He found a rhythm, using her own wetness to slick the way, to make the friction sweeter. He could tell she held her breath, her entire body tensed in expectation, and when she suddenly lurched and cried out he kissed her, swallowing the sound, taking it into himself. She forgot his instructions and wrapped her arms tightly around him, gripping him as if needing an anchor, as if she needed him as close as possible. Harry continued to kiss her, his tongue stroking in her mouth just as his finger stroked inside her. Her climax was long and full and she held him, her thighs rigid, her inner muscles trembling. She was so explosive, so *real*, he nearly lost control.

Making love to her, actually being inside her, might well kill him. But he was more than willing to take the risk.

As she quieted, he tenderly kissed her trembling lips. "You okay?"

She mumbled something he couldn't hear and burrowed a little closer.

"Should I take that as a yes?" He wanted to tease, but his voice shook and he knew he wouldn't last a minute longer.

For an answer, she bit him. He jumped, then rubbed his chest, though the small nip of her teeth hadn't really hurt. "Your vicious tendencies never cease to amaze me."

She gave him a scorching look and smiled. "My vicious tendencies will explode if you don't get on with it."

"Impatient wench." But he stood beside the bed and began unbuttoning his shirt. Charlie watched, lying on her back at her leisure, unashamed of her nudity or the sensual pose she presented.

Impossible as it seemed, her gaze grew even warmer and she breathed more deeply as he tossed his shirt aside and unbuttoned his slacks. He removed his wallet and pulled a condom from it, tossing it onto the nightstand beside her bed. She smiled.

Holding her gaze, he toed off his shoes, then pulled down his slacks, removing his shorts and socks at the same time. He straightened, then stood there, letting her look her fill.

She took a leisurely perusal of his body, from his shoulders all the way down to his feet. Once that was done, her gaze lifted to focus on his erection. He throbbed painfully, feeling her attention like a tactile touch.

"Well?"

With warm cheeks and hot eyes she nodded. "You'll do."

The laugh emerged as a bark, relieving a bit of his tension. He climbed back into bed with her. "Merely satisfactory, huh?"

"On the contrary." She crawled over him, lying along his length, propping her elbows on his chest. Her voice turned low and husky as she stared down into his eyes. "You're so incredibly sexy there are no words."

The breathless compliment pushed him right over the edge. "Charlie." He turned her beneath him and kissed her deeply, groaning at the acute sensation of her nakedness beneath him. With her arms free this time, she explored him, her small palms coasting over his shoulders, down his spine to his buttocks. He groaned again, then reared back. "Damn it. I'm sorry, but I can't wait. I wanted to make this last, to glut myself on you—"

"How romantic."

He shook his head, unable to banter with her at this moment when his need was so great. "I'll explode if I don't get inside you right now."

Her smile was pure female satisfaction. "So explode. I'm not stopping you."

Muttering another curse, he leaned over to the nightstand and grabbed the condom. Charlie watched in fascination as he put it on, then squealed when he quickly tucked her beneath him. "Put your legs around me."

She obeyed. He reached between their bodies, touching her, opening her for his thrust. "You're small, honey."

Her eyes were huge, watchful. "And you're not."

"No." He ground his teeth together while his fingers again explored her. Her feminine flesh was swelled, hot. And she was wet from her release. He closed his eyes. "I don't want to hurt you."

"It's all right, Harry. I won't break."

He wanted to laugh. Even now, she was full of bravado, unwilling to show any weakness. He wanted to wait, to ease into her gently, but she kept touching him and her hips squirmed against him. His control snapped. With a harsh curse, he entered her.

She caught her breath, but didn't fight him.

"Easy, sweetheart." He saw her through a red haze of overwhelming lust and tenderness, emotions that when mixed became volatile. She quivered, and her eyes closed, her neck arched. She gave a small moan, of pain or ecstasy, he couldn't tell. Then her legs tightened around his waist and her fingers tangled in his hair, and he was gone.

He rode her as gently as he could considering every muscle in his body strained for release. He felt sweat on his shoulders, felt her uneven breaths on his throat. And he felt Charlie, soft and inquisitive and delicate, despite the impression she liked to give the world.

Sliding one hand beneath her hips, he tilted her pelvis to allow him a deeper penetration, driven to bind their bodies together, to make her a part of him. She cried out, and her inner muscles clamped down on him.

"Come on, sweetheart," he ground out through his teeth, thrusting harder, faster, his control a distant memory. "Come for me again. I want you with me."

He felt the spasms in her legs first, then the way her entire body tensed. She caught and held her breath, her eyes squeezed tight, and she climaxed, holding him, whispering his name. Tears seeped past her lashes and as he joined her, his own release strong enough to steal his strength, the truth hit him. He loved her. Damn, how he loved her.

Now the real trouble would begin.

11

"OH HARRY. That was...indescribable."

She heard a grunt that could possibly pass for a reply, and grinned. Harry at a loss for words? What a novelty.

Her hands coasted over his slick shoulders and she kissed his throat. He tasted good. He smelled good. She admitted he *was* good. Her body still tingled pleasantly in very interesting places. "I wouldn't mind doing this again."

The grunt turned into a groan. With obvious effort, Harry raised his head. His light brown eyes were soft and sated and filled with some emotion she didn't understand.

He touched her hair, her cheek. "Insatiable, are we?"

"A tribute to your skill."

"Hmm. I suppose I could be convinced—in about an hour."

She laughed, then pushed at his shoulder. "In that case, you need to move. I have things to do."

Obediently, Harry rolled to the side, sprawling on his back like a vanquished warrior. When she started to crawl over him, he made a sound of appreciation and pulled her flat to his chest. "Don't you know lovers are supposed to talk after sex? It's callous to just use me and then leave the bed without any soft whispering and cuddling."

Toying with the hair on his chest, she laughed. "Callous, huh? I wouldn't want to be accused of that. But maybe we can talk later? I need to get going."

A frown appeared where before he'd been all smiles. "Where is it you think you have to rush off to?"

She tried to get up again, but now he had both hands cupping her bare backside, anchoring her in place. "I told you, I want to go keep an eye on Jill."

Harry closed his eyes with a soft curse. When he opened them again, she was struck by the cold determination there. "You don't need to do that."

"So says a man who doesn't have a little sister. Look, Harry, I know you said you checked up on Dalton. But how much could you have really found out? There could be all kinds of skeletons in his closet, and until I'm assured—"

"There aren't."

"You sound awfully sure of that." She watched him skeptically, knowing that particular tone and look.

With a sigh, Harry lifted her to the side of the bed and sat up. "We need to talk."

Charlie scrambled for the sheet and pulled it over her. "And we will. Later."

Resignation darkened his features as he glanced at her over his shoulder. "I know your father."

A strange foreboding made her stomach pitch. She pressed a fist to it and said logically, "Of course you do. You brought him here."

He waved her logic away. "I knew him before that.

I've known him for years." He turned to face her, still naked, his powerful shoulders gleaming in the lamplight, his dusty brown hair rumpled. His gaze never wavered from hers but tension emanated off him, pelting her with his resolution. "Dalton Jones has been like a father to me."

Feeling unsteady and sick, she moved away from him. She needed distance; she needed to be off the bed where they'd just made love. Backing up until she bumped into the dresser, she watched him. Harry never so much as flinched. "I don't understand."

"Dalton has looked for you for years, honey. He's suffered more than any one man ever should."

"You know him?" That one fact wouldn't quite penetrate.

Harry stood, too, but when she clutched her sheet tighter, he went still, making no move toward her. "My father was a cold, distant man who barely knew I existed. Dalton stepped in and did all the things for me that a father should do. He supported me in my decisions, and helped me get through my divorce from hell. He encouraged me and—"

"And did all the things for you that he didn't do for me." She felt lost, wounded to her soul.

"Not because he didn't care! He's spent a small fortune trying to locate you and Jill."

Not for anything would Charlie let him see how he'd hurt her, how her heart felt ready to break into pieces. She clutched at the sheet and tried to order her thoughts into some decipherable rationale. "Why didn't you tell me?"

Locking his jaw, Harry paced away, giving her a

distracting view of his muscled backside. It angered her that even now she was drawn to him, finding him irresistible.

He turned to face her and propped his hands on his hips. "I didn't know what the hell to do when you asked me to find your father. At the time, I felt my loyalty was to Dalton. It was his responsibility, his *pleasure*, to get to explain that he hadn't abandoned you. But you were so hostile about the whole thing, so...detached. You'd sent him that damn letter—"

"You knew about the letter?"

He gave a small nod. "I knew. Dalton told me that very night at the hospital. And he asked me not to tell you the truth yet, because he wanted a chance with you. He thought if I pretended to investigate him, I could give you a few facts that might soften you toward him."

That word *pretend* felt like a slap, bringing home just how much of her relationship with Harry was based on lies and manipulations. "So you played along?"

"Honey, I didn't know what else to do. I tried to talk him out of it, but he was afraid of losing you again."

"And of course, what he wanted is the only thing that mattered. I mean, you hardly know me really. I'm just..." She stopped in midsentence because she had no idea what she meant to Harry. Obviously not much or he couldn't have deceived her so easily. Needing something to do before she fell apart, she went to the closet and pulled out a T-shirt.

The bed creaked when Harry sat back down. "I'm so sorry, Charlie. I swear I never meant to hurt you."

She pulled clean jeans from the dresser, fighting off

the tears the best she could. "I understand. I don't like it, of course." The laugh, sounding close to hysteria, took her by surprise and she quickly suppressed it. "I feel pretty damn foolish, too. I can just imagine how the two of you must have been snickering. Especially after my stupid display tonight."

"No."

He started to get up, to come to her, but she warned him off with a bleak look. If he touched her, she'd sit down and cry like a baby, and that was something she hadn't done in too many years to count. "Don't even think it, Harry. The pretense is over."

Eyeing her rigid stance, he said carefully, "It wasn't all a pretense."

"No? Well, some day you'll have to tell me which parts came close to the truth. Right now, I'm just not interested. I'd like you to leave."

He swallowed hard, still watching her. "No."

"I need to get dressed!" The panic was real, making her voice too loud, too high. She needed to be alone. Already her hands were shaking and her legs were following suit.

"Charlie." Despite her warnings, he started toward her. She shook her head, but he looked more determined now than ever. "We have to talk about this."

"About how you used me? How you played along so Dalton wouldn't be disappointed?" His hands reached for her and her temper snapped. Without really thinking it through, she slapped him. Hard. The loud crack of her palm striking his handsome face sounded obscene. For an instant, they both froze. Then she covered her mouth, appalled.

Harry fingered his cheek, his brows up in surprise. "I didn't see that coming. Knowing you as I do, I was watching for a fist, or maybe a kick. Not a feminine slap."

"*Don't you dare tease me now.*"

"I'm sorry. But Charlie, there's more I have to tell you."

"Oh?" Her stomach clenched, but she forced herself to be flippant. "Did you maybe just fake what we did in bed?"

Incredulous, he stared at her a moment, then laughed. "Honey, men can't fake a thing like that."

Her teeth ground together. "You know what I mean. And don't call me honey."

He hesitated for the briefest moment. "No, I didn't fake it." His gaze softened, turned intimate, and he whispered, "I love you."

Her chest hurt so much she gasped. She felt raw and exposed, and she almost hated him. *Almost.* "Did Dalton tell you to say that? To do whatever was necessary to appease me?"

"No."

In a burst of temper, she snapped, "Will you at least put some damn clothes on!"

His expression didn't change. "Dalton had a heart attack the day you sent the letter." He caught her before she dropped to the floor, then led her to the bed. He spoke quickly now, rushing his words together. "I was so worried about him, it's part of the reason I let him talk me into this harebrained plan, because I didn't want to see him disappointed again. You've been so hurt, I couldn't guess how you might react to the truth, if you'd even give Dalton a chance. And if you didn't, with his health in danger—"

She was back off the bed in a flash, no longer worried about her sheet or keeping her body covered. She jerked on her jeans and pulled the T-shirt over her head, then stepped into a pair of sneakers.

"Charlie—"

She rounded on him. "You bastard!" Stepping close so she could shake a fist in his face, she yelled, "My father could have died, and you didn't tell me?"

He caught and held her fists. "He's fine now, Charlie. He only needs to be more cautious."

She shoved him away then turned for the door. Harry grabbed her shoulder. "Where are you going?"

"To see him. I want you out of my place." She picked up a key off the dresser and flung it at him. "Let yourself out."

"Wait!" He started rushing into his own clothes. "I'll go with you."

"Ha!"

"It's not safe, Charlie! Damn it, you don't know what's going on!"

But she was already hurrying down the hall. Harry tried to follow after her, and she barely slipped through the door in time. She heard his fist hit it with incredible force, and he yelled her name again. She ignored him. She knew by the time he got the key and unlocked the door, she'd be gone. And if she never saw him again, it was only what she deserved.

CHARLIE CHECKED first at Maria's, the restaurant where they'd planned to eat, but Dalton and her sister weren't there. She assumed they had gone on to Dalton's jewelry store, so she headed in that direction. At the moment, she had no idea what she planned to say to her father, but she needed to reassure herself that he was okay. Whether he cared about her or not, he was her father, and that mattered. It mattered more than she'd ever thought possible, and she now regretted all her plans for revenge. It made her almost sick to think she might have played a part in his ill health with her hurtful letter.

All her concentration was centered on the problem with her father. She couldn't think about Harry. If she did, she might start bawling like a baby. She loved the arrogant, obnoxious jerk, and yet he'd used her. The really sad part was, she could understand his reasons for the deception. In his position, she might have done the same. And if she hadn't pushed so hard, their relationship probably wouldn't have become intimate. She had only herself to blame. She'd been a complete fool—and she'd behaved like her mother. The truth hurt so bad she didn't think she could stand it.

She trudged up the sidewalk to the jewelry store, lost in thought. At first she didn't notice when a car pulled up beside her. Absently, she turned to look, and was stunned to see Floyd in the passenger seat, grinning at her with evil intent. The car stopped and she broke into a dead run, but she'd only gotten a few feet before he caught her arm and jerked her back. She stumbled, going down hard on one knee. She groaned at the jarring pain.

The car pulled alongside and Ralph got out. "Get her in the back seat."

Hearing that cleared the pain from her knee enough to allow her to fight. She started kicking and shouting, doing anything she could to fend them off. Somehow she knew if they got her in the car, she might never get out again.

Floyd managed to drag her as far as the curb, using her arm and her shirt collar for leverage. Even in her struggle, she saw the unfamiliar man in the front seat. She had the brief impression of a polished businessman before shouts sounded behind her. Her blood nearly froze when she recognized Dalton's voice.

"No!" He couldn't get into a skirmish because of her, not with his heart condition. If anything happened to him... She doubled her efforts, and caught Floyd low in the stomach with a fist. He grunted and loosened his hold. She tried to roll away, but Ralph reached for her.

"Let her go!" Dalton leaped onto Ralph's back, knocking him down, all the while cursing so vividly Charlie couldn't help but be impressed. The third man in the car got out and started toward them with a purposeful stride.

Suddenly other men were there, leaving their shops in a rush, leaping into the fray, crowding together on the sidewalk. It became a chaotic free-for-all with the elderly swinging canes and brooms and fists. Vile threats filled the air from both factions. Charlie was tossed aside and landed on her butt, but she was back up in a heartbeat when she saw the man from the car reach inside his jacket. *Oh God, a gun!*

Dalton threw himself in front of her, and no matter how she tried, she couldn't get around him. The brawl ended, no one daring to move. Floyd and Ralph, with a lot of blustering, brushed themselves off and straightened their jackets. Six older men and two gray-haired women stood in a circle, their hands in fists, their faces red.

"What should we do with them all, Carlyle?"

Carlyle. Again, Charlie strained to see around Dalton's shoulder, curious about the man Harry wanted so badly. After being kidnapped and harassed, she owed Carlyle much, and now with him threatening her father her rage grew.

She ducked under Dalton's arm, but before she could take two steps Harry was there. In a flash, he was around the parked car, jerking Carlyle's hand up so the gun fired in the air with a loud crack of sound, and wrapping one long muscled arm around his throat, squeezing tight enough to make Carlyle's eyes bug. Sirens whined in the distance.

Ralph and Floyd started to back up, but they were quickly subdued by the older folk. Floyd screeched like a wet hen when his arm was twisted high, and Moses, with a look of disgust, muttered, "Sissy."

Pops stepped forward and wagged a fist. "Shoot 'em!"

Harry's gaze met Charlie's, and he smiled. "He's as bloodthirsty as you are, brat."

Carlyle lurched, trying to break free, and without a single hesitation, Harry punched him the jaw. The man went down like a lead balloon. Very slowly, Charlie applauded.

The police showed up in two patrol cars and a plain sedan. The detective in charge appeared to know

Harry. With the men subdued in cuffs, the trunk of Carlyle's car was opened and Charlie glimpsed a variety of weapons, rifles and guns and ammunition. There were so many of them, it looked like an arsenal.

One of the officers whistled low.

"They're dealing in illegal and stolen weaponry." Charlie noticed Harry didn't mention the embezzlement, keeping to his promise not to involve the older proprietors. "I can give you an address of an abandoned warehouse where you'll find more of the same, as well as evidence of other illegal activities."

The detective clapped Harry on the shoulder and they spoke quietly for a few minutes. The officers were questioning everyone and to Charlie's surprise, the seniors loved it. They fairly crowed in their excitement. Charlie used the moment to go to Dalton.

"Where's my sister?"

He was still catching his breath, but he looked relieved. "Inside. My assistant is practically sitting on her. She wanted to rush out with me, but seeing you threatened was more than enough." He touched her face and his hand trembled. Charlie took his arm and hustled him to a shop stoop to sit. Even as he did her bidding, he asked, "Are you okay?"

She smiled. At the same time big tears welled in her eyes. "That was my question to you."

"Now that you're safe, I'm fine. But I don't mind telling you, seeing that bastard put his hands on you nearly stopped my—"

"Your heart?" She knelt down in front of him and took his hands. "Are you sure you're all right?"

"You know?"

"That you had a heart attack? Yes. Harry finally came clean."

Dalton sighed heavily. "It wasn't your fault, you know. Your letter didn't distress me. It thrilled me and made me so proud I wanted to dance up and down the street."

"It was a hateful letter."

"It was a letter filled with guts and courage and pride. I knew the moment I read it you were an incredible young woman. I was right."

The tears trickled down her cheeks and she impatiently swiped them away. "That was a dirty trick you played on me, having Harry lie about everything. But under the circumstances I suppose I understand."

"Do you? I couldn't take the chance you'd shut me out. I'd waited too long to get my girls back." His own eyes teared up, breaking Charlie's heart. "I'm so sorry I hurt you earlier today."

She shook her head. "It doesn't matter."

"That's not what Harry said. I've known him since he was a boy, back when his father and I were friends. We've always been as close as two men can be, and that's the first time he ever raised hell with me."

Once again, her temper rose. "Harry yelled at you?"

Scoffing, Dalton shook his head. "Harry never yells. He just gets glib and lectures. He told me what a wonderful woman you were, and he insisted there wasn't a single thing about you that needed to be changed."

Charlie was absorbing that when a voice from behind her said, "What I didn't tell you is that I love her."

She jerked around so fast, she landed on her rump.

Since that particular part of her anatomy was already sore from the skirmish, she scowled at Harry. He didn't give her a chance to grumble, reaching down and grabbing her under her arms, then lifting her completely off her feet until she was eye level, dangling in the air.

Charlie gulped, eyeing Harry cautiously. His shirt was untucked and only half-buttoned, and he had on shoes but no socks. He'd obviously dressed in a rush.

Shaking her slightly, he shouted, "You scared the hell out of me, taking off like that!"

Charlie glanced over at Dalton, who sat there grinning, and she said, "I thought he never yelled."

Dalton shrugged.

Harry shook her again, making her feet swing. "In the normal course of things, when not unduly provoked, I *don't* yell! But you have a way of pushing me on everything."

Despite her ignominious position, she lifted her chin. "Good. Because you push me, too."

That vexed him for a moment, and he growled, "Damn right! And I'm going to continue to do so. I love you, damn it. Doesn't that matter at all?"

Pops leaned in to say, "It should matter."

Moses nodded. "Always used to matter in the good ole days." The rest of the seniors offered mumbled agreements.

An elderly woman with gray hair escaping her bun patted Charlie on the arm. "You should listen to him, honey. Harry's a good man, and he packs one helluva punch."

They all nodded, even the officers. Moses stepped

forward and he looked sheepish. "Harry convinced us we couldn't handle those punks on our own. We should have trusted the cops. Even outnumberin' 'em two to one, they almost got away from us."

Harry, still holding Charlie off the ground as if her weight were totally negligible, said to the hovering group, "I couldn't have done it without your assistance."

Charlie frowned. "It was a plan?"

"A very sound plan. I knew Carlyle would be with Ralph and Floyd today, and I knew they'd have the guns."

Charlie gasped. "This is the news you refused to share with me! I suspected something was going on, but you wouldn't tell me a damn thing, and you kept sneaking off without me—"

"Which wasn't easy, I'll have you know. You're too nosy for your own good."

Dalton blustered. "*Charlie* was involved in that?"

Harry didn't answer, however his eyes glittered. "After picking up the money, they were going to make a deal—and the police would be ready." He glared at Dalton. "Things would have gone as planned if people didn't throw wrenches into the works, skipping dinner and coming here first."

"I had no idea!" He frowned at Harry, then shrugged. "I needed a reservation, so we were going back in an hour."

"And," Harry added, drawing Charlie so close she could see the fiery specks in his light brown eyes, "if stubborn women would only listen when given a heartfelt declaration of love."

"It really was heartfelt?"

"Haven't you been listening?" He shook her again, then hugged her tight. "It was extremely heartfelt."

Charlie looped her arms around his neck. "I haven't forgiven you yet for lying to me."

Harry pulled her slightly away and he looked at Dalton. "I compromised your daughter."

Dalton started in surprise. "You did?"

"Yes. But I'm willing to do the right thing."

The old people cheered all the more.

Charlie, enjoying herself now that she no longer doubted her father—or Harry—pretended to think things over. "I'm going to keep my bar."

"Fine. As long as you live with me."

"What about Jill?"

"She's more than welcome as long as she doesn't object to Ted, or Grace and Sooner."

Dalton stood. "Or she could live with me!"

Jill appeared, dragging the assistant in her wake. Several of the young officers looked at her with interest as she forged a path to her sister. "I'm going off to college, remember? But it's nice to feel so wanted. Who're Ted and Grace and Sooner?"

Harry brought Charlie close again and kissed her. In a whisper, he said, "I do love you, Charlie. So damn much. Please don't ever scare me like that again."

Those stupid, ridiculous tears threatened, but they were happy tears now. "If I marry you, can I help in all your investigations?"

He pretended to stagger with the mere thought, making her laugh. But that was the thing about Harry. Even from the first, he'd managed to bring fun and laughter back into her life. He'd even given her back her father. And now that she had those things, she couldn't imagine letting them go.

She pressed her face into his throat and said, "Since I love you, I suppose we should get married."

"That's a yes?"

"That's an absolute."

Sirens from the retreating patrol cars mingled with the shouts from the seniors and the happy shrieks from her sister. Dalton just sat there grinning—like a very proud papa.

HARLEQUIN®
Temptation.

**They're sexy. They're single.
And they're Southern!
They're...**

Sweet Talkin' Guys

Early this year, Temptation is chasing away the
winter blues by bringing you the South's most
irresistible bad boys.

Watch for:

#768 BARING IT ALL by Sandra Chastain
available January 2000

#769 IT TAKES A REBEL by Stephanie Bond
available February 2000

#773 SOUTHERN COMFORTS by Sandy Steen
available March 2000

Don't miss upcoming stories by Donna Sterling,
Lyn Ellis and Heather MacAllister.

*Sweet Talkin' Guys—
All talk and all action!*

Available at your favorite retail outlet.

HARLEQUIN®
Makes any time special™

Visit us at www.romance.net

HTSTG

If you enjoyed what you just read,
then we've got an offer you can't resist!

Take 2 bestselling
love stories FREE!

Plus get a FREE surprise gift!